Alfred Austin

Jessie's Expiation

Vol. 3

Alfred Austin

Jessie's Expiation
Vol. 3

ISBN/EAN: 9783337258221

Printed in Europe, USA, Canada, Australia, Japan

Cover: Foto ©Andreas Hilbeck / pixelio.de

More available books at **www.hansebooks.com**

JESSIE'S EXPIATION.

𝔄 𝔑𝔬𝔳𝔢𝔩.

BY

OSWALD BOYLE.

IN THREE VOLUMES.

VOL. III.

LONDON:

TINSLEY BROTHERS, 18, CATHERINE STREET, STRAND.

1867.

CONTENTS

OF

THE THIRD VOLUME.

JESSIE'S EXPIATION.

CHAPTER I.

IN THE TOILS OF THE HUNTER.

ABOUT noon of the following day, Lord Rendover was sitting in his study. He had already written two or three letters, and these were lying, addressed, on the table. One of them was for " Percy Carryngton, Esquire, Jermyn Street."

He took up *The Times.* He was not a very great newspaper reader; but since the Leverstoke petition had been going on, he had followed the reports of the sittings of the Committee with care and regularity. He read to-day's report all through, seemed thoroughly well satisfied with it, and was just going to put down the paper when his eye lighted on a name which immediately attracted his attention, and caused him to peruse the paragraph in which it figured. The paragraph, inserted in a corner, ran thus—

"DARING ESCAPE FROM GAOL.—The public will scarcely have forgotten the particulars of an audacious burglary committed in the autumn of last year at Fleetwood Manse. Two of the prisoners were convicted at the spring assizes, mainly through the evidence of a confederate who turned informer against them, and were sentenced to penal servitude for life. Within less than five months they have contrived to escape from confinement, and have as yet baffled all the efforts of the police to recapture them. They have the reputation of being exceedingly desperate fellows, and the way in which they effected their release speaks but too plainly not only for their boldness but their ingenuity."

It was not a light matter that could make Lord Rendover change colour. For-

tunately for him he was alone, and there
was accordingly no one to witness the pal-
lor which now unquestionably overspread
his features.   He very soon recovered
his wonted aspect, however, put down the
paper, and sat back in his chair, thinking.

"All the more reason for settling that
tiresome business somehow.   Obstinate
little brute!   I wish Percy had taken a
fancy to her.   But there's nothing to be
hoped for in that direction.   And not only
will he not serve me in any way; but if
that woman's right—and they nearly
always are right in such matters—he positively is trying to balk me in what he ·
knows well enough I am determined to do.
But I can cut *his* claws for him, at any
moment.   I wonder what he'll say to that
letter.   By —, one thing's certain.   He
shan't marry her.   But"— and he laughed
at his own burst of wrath—"how absurd !
As if there was the slightest chance.
People flirt, and sigh, and do what they
call love each other.   But it all means

nothing where there is nothing solid. I believe people can love on air, but I'll be hanged if they can marry on it!"

Again he sat silent, and pondered. Then he folded the newspaper and put it in his pocket—a most unusual thing for him to do.

"Better that Thornton should not see it, if it can be avoided; he's such a cur. I wonder what time there's a Windsor train."

He was just going to rise and ring the bell, when there was a knock at the door, and Thornton entered with a letter, which had come by hand, and on which was written "Immediate."

"Mr. Chichester Fleetwood's servant is waiting for an answer, my lord. Shall he do so?"

"Yes. I will ring when I am ready."

Thornton left the room. Lord Rendover opened the letter and read:—

"DEAR RENDOVER—
"I am sorry that anything unpleasant

should have occurred between us last night. But I know you are too much a man of the world to expect me to say anything more about it; and I may at once go on to the matter which is the real object of this letter.

"Do you object to our cancelling our Goodwood bet? I see by this morning's papers that the betting in Philister's favour is considerably improved since yesterday, and therefore the chances of my winning are very materially increased. It is, however, a very large bet for a man of my moderate means to make, and it was made in great haste. I should therefore much prefer to be off it, and should feel myself under an obligation to you if you will consent to my proposal.

"Yours faithfully,

"CHICHESTER FLEETWOOD."

Rendover drew the paper out of his pocket, and looked at Goodwood quotations, which he had not glanced at before, not anticipating any alterations.

"True enough. Our bet was nine to five, and now the odds are eight to five, and they seem to think he'll win easily. Then why can Fleetwood want to be off it? For no other reason that I conceive, but that, if he happens to lose, it will be a desperately awkward thing for him. But that's precisely what I offered it to him for. No, damme, I'll risk it. If he loses, there's an end of him, as far as the Beauty's concerned; and if he wins, I don't think it would mend his chance with old Blessington very much."

He took up his pen and wrote:—

"DEAR FLEETWOOD—

"I had quite forgotten the momentary altercation to which you refer. With regard to the bet, I do not see that I can close with your offer, handsome though it is. We must stick to the bargain, of which you now seem to have much the best. If you win, I shall be the first to

congratulate you on your good fortune.
We shall meet at Goodwood.

"Yours faithfully,

"RENDOVER."

He rang the bell, and Thornton again
appeared.

"There is the answer. I want you as
soon you have given it to Mr. Fleetwood's
servant."

"Yes, my lord."

In a moment he had returned to his
lordship's study.

"I want to know, Thornton, precisely
what occurred when you were last at the
cottage. You told me before, I know, but
I have forgotten, and want just to hear it
again."

"Well, my lord, you know how anxious
she was to hear of those old folks near
Dipleydale, and how particularly she
wanted me to see somebody or other in
those parts, and make out for her what they
seemed to be saying about her down there."

"Just so. And you told her that you had heard all about it."

"Yes, my lord, I made believe that I had been at Dipleydale, and into the stationer's shop there, and how I had heard that the old folks she used to live with had given her up altogether, and wanted to hear nothing more about her."

"And she seemed to see that it was no use her thinking of going back."

"Just that, my lord. She didn't say much; she never does. But it was evident she thought it was no use."

"Very well. That was all I wanted to know. What's the next train to Windsor? Or the next but one?"

Thornton soon returned with the information, and his lordship said that was all he wanted, and Thornton might go. The latter, however, seemed to linger, arranged something in the room which did not visibly want any fresh arranging, walked to the door, opened it, held the handle, coughed so as to attract Lord Rendover's attention, closed the door again gently, and began—

"I hope your lordship 'll excuse the liberty I take."

"Yes, certainly, what is it?" said his lordship, as rapidly as Thornton had spoken slowly and hesitatingly.

"I was only thinking, my lord, that if it should so be that your lordship wishes to be rid of that little affair altogether, and not be—not be, what shall I say, my lord? —not be bothered any more about it, I myself had a notion which perhaps your lordship might—I only say, *might*, my lord —your lordship might possibly think not a bad one."

"And what is it, Thornton?" asked Lord Rendover, with some little curiosity.

"I always want to be in your service, my lord, and I hope your lordship will always understand that," said Thornton, apologetically.

"Perfectly," rejoined Lord Rendover, significantly. "That is quite agreed between us."

"Just so, my lord; and the scheme I propose would not interfere with that, if I only succeed in explaining myself rightly. But I *was* thinking that if it could so be that your lordship had no objections, I might marry her myself, my lord, and then, you know, my lord, there would be an end of the matter."

Once having expressed himself of his views, Mr. Richard Thornton, however much during this process he had been changing his feet and manifesting his hesitation by the irregular movements of his hands, now fell into a perfectly quiescent attitude, and stood, if not erect or particularly firm, in a position of tranquil self-control which ought to have been dignified but was exceedingly ludicrous. Lord Rendover had a good sense of humour, and it was not very easy for his countenance to preserve the requisite gravity. He leaned his head upon his hand, thereby hiding his amusement and seeming to be struck by the suggestion at the same time.

"Well, Thornton," he said at last, taking away his hand and rising from his chair, "there's something in what you say. I'll think about it, and see if it can be managed. There'll be some difficulty in any case; but you've been an uncommonly lucky dog so far, and I don't see why you should not have another good stroke of fortune. But you must not count upon it. However, as I say, I'll think it over."

"Thank you, my lord. I'm sure it would be a very good plan, if once your lordship agreed to it, and it 'ud be a good thing for everybody. There never could be any more bother. I should be thoroughly well pleased, my lord; and as for her, she'd be married, and it 'ud be a respectable position for her, and a sort of reparation, my lord, your lordship knows, for any little trouble she may have had. And I think she's had a little—just a little, perhaps."

"Very well, Thornton. That will do. The carriage in twenty minutes."

Three hours later, or rather less, Lord

Rendover was at the cottage. His visit was unexpected by its occupant; but she was there to receive him. She was more plainly dressed than he had ever seen her since he used to meet her in the Dipleydale Woods, and her face wore an aspect of hard settled resolve such as was quite new, and such as he could not fail to observe. He made no comment, however, upon either fact.

After salutations of a nature precisely similar to previous ones, which we once saw in the same spot, he at once began—

"I came down here to tell you that I want you to leave the cottage and live somewhere else."

"Yes," she answered, quietly. "Where?"

"I want you to live in London. I have taken a house for you there."

"I will not live in London," she answered, quietly. "I have told you that before, and you know it."

"And for a time I have chosen to humour you. But this state of things cannot last.   I cannot have you living here any longer."

"I will move to any other place in the country you like.   I do not care how small or poor it is.   Any sort of a cottage will do for me.   But it must be in the country, and quite away from people."

"But I don't want you to live in a small or poor cottage," he answered.   "You might do me the justice to own that not only have I never wanted you to live, but I never would hear of your living, in any such way. It is by your own choice that you are here in this little place.   I have tried to make it as nice and comfortable as possible, but I have always wanted to provide you with something very much larger and better."

"I want nothing better, and I have always told you so—at least ever since you refused to do justice by me.   It is too large and too good already, and more than I have any pretension to.   But I will leave it to-morrow, if you wish.   I have no liking for it." Her voice waxed lower but deeper and more intense. "I hate it."

"Now, Jessie, that sort of thing will do no good. I have come here to talk reasonably and quietly to you, and it's no use your getting into a passion."

"I am not in a passion. I am ready to listen to anything you may have to say."

"Then will you live in London?"

"No, I will not."

"I will give you a beautiful house there, and as much to keep it up, and keep yourself on, as you can desire. You will also have your horse there, just as you have here."

"I have not got a horse here any longer," she said.

"What do you mean? You have not got a horse? Where has it gone to?"

"I ordered the man to sell it, and I have got the money for you in my desk. I will go and get it."

"Nonsense! Stay here. And what may all this mean; this selling of your horse, without saying a word to *me*?"

" You have not been here for some time, and I was determined henceforth to take nothing from you but what is absolutely necessary to me, and I did not choose to wait till you might happen to come, so I sold the horse at once, and I have made up all your presents into a parcel, and if you do not choose to take them away, I will bury them in the garden, only I wont keep them, that's all. I will leave the cottage whenever you like, but I will not go to London; and still less will I go to a beautiful house in London. I will have nothing beautiful from you of any kind, either here or anywhere else. And now you know."

" This is simply ridiculous. However absurdly you may wish to act, you cannot expect me to act in the same way."

" You can act as you like, but so will I. I will be mistress of myself as far as I can, and you may make what other arrangements you think proper. But I will not go to London, and I will not live like a lady, when I'm not one."

"But, Jessie, you are a lady."

"No, I am not. You said you would make me one, and you have not done so. I don't want you to do so now. I know now that you do not care for me in the least, and therefore I will take nothing from you but what you are bound to give me; the food and shelter you took from me."

"But I want to give you far more than these."

"And I will not take them, and I tell you that now, once for all. Either help me to go back home, or give me some place with just one woman to live with me, in order that I may not be quite alone, and give us enough money for ever to prevent us from starving, and then never come near us, for I never want to see you again."

"I will not be so unjust," he said. "I will never leave you in any such condition."

"Then help me to go back home, to go back to Dipleydale, to Netwold Farm, to Uncle Roger, to Aunt Mary—to everybody."

In an instant her manner had wholly

altered. She had risen from her seat. She had exchanged her hard, cold, resolute tone for one of tender pathetic pleading. The idea that had been nestling in her heart all these months, had at length fluttered up to her lips, and she no longer strove to restrain it. She looked as though she would almost throw herself at Rendover's feet. She came close to him, closer than she had been for many a long time, till she almost touched him.

"Help me to go back. Make it possible for me to go back. I ask for nothing else; I want nothing else. I know you do not care for me, and I—I do not want you to do. I never want to see or hear of you again. But I will forgive everything—I will like you again, I will try to think kindly of you, I will be grateful to you, if you will only help me to go back home, and make me just as I was before you dragged me violently away from it."

"I do not prevent you from going back," he said, "though I think it would be very foolish of you to attempt to go back to people who, you may be sure, do not want you."

"They do not want me, because they believe lies of me, and only you can tell them the truth, and how it all was, and how I was not what they say of me, no good, but only weak and foolish and unfortunate. You did it all, you know you did. Why will you not undo it? Are you afraid? I swear nothing shall be done by anybody. Only go to Netwold, and tell them the truth, the real truth, and. then I shall be able to go back. And get those wicked men who helped you, and make them go with you, and let them tell the whole truth too, and Uncle Roger will believe it, I am sure, and then Aunt Mary will believe it, and everybody will believe it, and all will be as before, and you will be quite free and never bothered with me any more. But unless you do that, I can do nothing. They would not believe me alone. They say I am no good, and never

was—never was—no good——" And she
fell back into the chair, and burst out
crying, and sobbed as if her heart would
break.

Lord Rendover walked to the window
and looked out. It was a sultry afternoon
at the very end of July, and the sky was
waxing dark and heavy with thunder-clouds.
A storm was evidently gathering. He had
only an open carriage. He would very
likely be caught in it before he could get
back to Windsor. He wished she would
give up blubbering. As soon as the sound
of sobbing ceased, he turned to her again.

" Now, Jessie, you know that nothing of
the kind is possible. They would believe
me no more than they would believe you,
and they would merely regard it as a plot
concocted by both of us. It would do no
good, and might do a deal of mischief."

" Then marry me," she said. "Marry
me as you said you would, and then I will
go back alone. I could go back then, for I
could say that I was married, and show

them that I was, and then they would take
me in and be kind to me as before. I do
not want to be your wife: I only want you
to marry me in a church and then to let me
go.   You can do whatever you like afterwards, and I will never bother you or come
near you again, and you shall never hear of
me, or of Uncle Roger, or of Aunt Mary, or
anybody.   Only do something by which I
shall be able to go back to them, without
their shutting the door in my face, or letting
me in and thinking of me what they think
now.   Will you, will you?"

He walked up and down the room,
pondering upon something, whilst the first
thunder-peals growled from afar. At length
he said—

"Will you marry—not me, but somebody
else?"

"Yes — anybody — anybody," she answered, clutching at a ray of hope.

"Do you promise?" he asked, gravely.

"Yes—yes—I promise. I will marry
anybody—anybody. Only he must not be

wicked: that is all. And do not let it be anybody who is very cruel! Please, nobody who is cruel. He will not be cruel, or wicked, will he? Tell me, he will not."

" No, he shall be neither. He shall treat you properly. But mind, you have promised me."

" Yes, I know I have, and I will, I will marry him. Only you have promised me that he shall not be cruel to me."

" Just so. And now, good-bye. I must get away, if possible, before the storm comes."

But it was too late. The first heavy drops were falling. He ran across the garden, jumped into the carriage, and drove away. But the sound of the receding wheels was drowned in a loud clap of thunder, and the big direct rain came down in pitiless torrents.

CHAPTER II.

THE Goodwood Races were over. After the storm which burst on the afternoon of the day that Rendover was at the cottage, the weather had remained broken, and the course was in a state which upset all previous calculations. Philister could do nothing over the heavy sloppy ground, and was almost nowhere. Dismay was spread among his backers, and Chichester Fleetwood had lost his bet.

Nobody had seen him on the course that day; but the first thing that was put into Lord Rendover's hands, on waking the morning after the race, was a letter from him, marked "Private and Confidential." It ran thus:

" Dear Rendover—

"You will now understand why I wanted to be off my bet. At the exact moment of making it, I had every reason to believe, not only that I was well able to pay if I lost, but that in a few days my means would be such as to make me, if I lost, scarcely feel the loss at all. I had gone into a speculation, for going into which my former experiences in the East, with which you are acquainted, had fully qualified me, and from which I, and everybody who knew anything about it, believed that I should reap considerable gain. Things have turned out quite differently, indeed most disastrously; and I am forced to acquaint you that, even by leaving myself without a shilling in the world, I shall still be unable to pay you at once more than ten out of the forty thousand pounds I owe you.

"Will you allow the thirty thousand pounds to stand over till I can pay you, meanwhile accepting my acknowledgment— all I can offer you—for the debt, and not

letting it be known that I have not yet paid
you? I should so be preserved from a dishonour that I cannot feel I have deserved.
If you consent, I shall of course at once
devote my energies to putting myself in a
position to extricate myself from the liability,
though the obligation will always remain.

" I am yours faithfully,

"CHICHESTER FLEETWOOD."

"Was there ever such a piece of luck?"
exclaimed Rendover, as he refolded the
letter. "This is a matter not to be decided
in a hurry. It may turn out exceedingly
useful. Meanwhile, I must drop him a line,
I suppose."

He wrote thus briefly:

"DEAR FLEETWOOD—

"I beg to acknowledge the
receipt of your letter, and will give it a
definitive reply as soon as possible.

"Yours faithfully,

"RENDOVER."

"And now," he said, drawing himself up to his full height—"now for the last coup of all. This last wonderful piece of luck has cleared the ground amazingly. And as for Master Percy—by-the-bye, I wonder he has not written—I think that note of mine will have brought him to his senses, and shown him how powerless he is without me at his back."

"The last coup of all" was nothing less than Lord Rendover's formal proposal to Gertrude Blessington, which he had yester-day at Goodwood arranged with Mr. Blessington should take place at the squire's house this very day.

Gertrude, however, was—as it will be remembered she told Percy she should be— at Mrs. Grantley Morris's. Thither Car-ryngton had sent her, enclosed in another envelope, the note which we saw lying for him on Rendover's table, but with whose contents we have not been yet made acquainted. They were to the following effect:

"DEAR PERCY—

"You have shown yourself so unwilling to co-operate with me in any scheme of mine for your advancement, that it would be unreasonable of you to expect me to continue to take the same interest in your career as I have hitherto done. I shall not withdraw the allowance that I have made you, if you think proper still to take it, and I enclose a cheque for £400, a half-year now due. But I do not pledge myself in any way to secure it to you, neither must you count upon it at my death. I am sorry this should be so; but I am bound to say the fault lies entirely with you.

"Yours sincerely,

"RENDOVER."

Percy had not been able to send this note to Miss Blessington immediately, inasmuch as he knew that she had not yet gone to Mrs. Morris's. He sent it the first day that he felt certain it would find her, and along with it he wrote just these few lines:

"Dear Miss Blessington—

"Will you kindly read and consider the enclosed, so that when I call this afternoon, you may be in a position to tell me if your view of what should be my conduct under the circumstances agrees with my own?

"Yours most sincerely,
"Percy Carryngton."

In the afternoon, accordingly, he went and made his call. He found Mrs. Morris, but no Gertrude.

"Gertrude left me quite unexpectedly this morning," the fair hostess said to him. "She told me that she believed you were coming to see us to-day, and asked me to tell you how sorry she was that she should not see you. I expect her here again to-morrow, however; for she has promised to stay a week with me."

"And where has she gone to?" he asked.

"Only home. Her papa wanted to see her, she said."

Percy stayed a quarter of an hour, and then took his leave, desperately disappointed at not seeing her, and determined to make another attempt on the following afternoon. He was burning to answer Rendover's letter, yet did not like to do so until he had the advice of her who, he knew, could never advise him wrongly.

The reason for Gertrude being so suddenly sent for can now easily be guessed. Early in the morning—the morning after Goodwood—Squire Blessington had informed his wife of the arrangement which he had made with Lord Rendover on the course the pre·· ceding afternoon.

"Dear, dear," said Mrs. Blessington, "how annoying! Gertrude went to the Morrises only yesterday evening, intending to spend a few days with them. I wish I had known sooner."

"What does it matter?" answered the blunt squire. "She can be sent for. Write a note, and send for her at once."

"Yes, that can be done, if you wish it,"

remarked his wife, with a certain amount of hesitation in her tone.

"If I wish it!" said the squire, testily. "I tell you that I wish it, and not only that I wish it, but that I have made a positive arrangement with Rendover for him to see her here at four o'clock."

"Very well, my dear, I will see to it at once. But I hope Lord Rendover is not acting too precipitately."

"What do you mean," asked the squire, "by acting too precipitately?"

"You know, my dear," pleaded Mrs. Blessington, meekly, "I can have no other wish on the subject but what you have, and therefore it is that I do not want our wishes to be crossed through any undue haste. I do not feel at all sure that Gertrude is ready for any formal proposal to be made to her by Lord Rendover."

"Not ready! Not ready! Then she ought to be ready. The man has spent the whole season in courting her and paying her attention. What the deuce can the girl want more ?   I think Rendover has behaved admirably.   I could not have wished him to behave better—I could not have behaved better myself. Not ready ! How do you know she's not ready?   Has she said so?"

" No, she has not said so.   Indeed, she has said nothing, as not a word has passed between us on the subject."

" Then, I think a word might have passed between you, and a good many words.   I should like to know what a mother is made for, if not to influence her daughter's mind to do her duty."

" But, my dear George, Gertrude is a girl of such a high spirit, that I feared to do more harm than good by speaking to her before I saw a favourable moment for doing so.   And I did not think she was ready to be spoken to, even by me, especially as she never had offered to speak of it her-self."

" I think you have shown a great lack of judgment, and, I must say, incapacity for managing Gertrude. You surely," he added, abruptly, "you surely have no reason to suppose that she is hankering after that other fellow?"

"Do you mean Mr. Chichester Fleetwood?" suggested Mrs. Blessington, mildly.

"Yes, of course I do. Do you suppose she cares for him?"

"I have no reason to think so, I am sure."

"Then of course she's ready to marry Rendover. Stuff and nonsense! Not ready! The whole thing's absurd. But you take such a ridiculous and weak view of the case, and you have so thoroughly mismanaged it —indeed, you have done nothing that I can see—that I had better take it into my own hands, and do it all myself. *I'll* send for Gertrude. Never you mind writing, I'll settle it all; I'll settle it all."

And away went the testy, despotic old fellow to his study, leaving poor Mrs. Blessington exceedingly consoled at having the matter taken out of her hands. She felt it to be very doubtful, however, if he

would succeed any better than she herself
would, and she knew, moreover, that his
failure, if he did fail, would be visited upon
her all the same.   She would, however,
meanwhile gather up strength to encounter
the rebukes which would in such case
inevitably fall to her lot.

The squire was very direct in his management of affairs, whenever he took them into
his own hands.   He knew and cared nothing
about tact, compromise, delay.   He knew
only how to give a command, and be obeyed.
Now, moreover, he was resolved to go
straight to his point all the more, because
his wife had so miserably failed in her duty.
His note to his daughter contained nothing
more than

"MY DEAR GERTRUDE—
          "Come home at once.   I want
you.
          "Your affectionate Father."

Having written it, he quietly awaited her

arrival, without even giving himself the trouble to consider what precisely he should say to her when she did come. The matter seemed to him so exceedingly simple.

He had of course sent the carriage for her, and he happened to hear it drive up to the front door on its return.

"How are you, papa dear?" she said, meeting him in the hall, and going up to him and kissing him. "What did you want me so very particularly for, that you sent for me to-day?"

"Come in here, my child, and I will tell you."

She followed him into his study, at the back of the dining-room, without taking off her things, and closed the door after her.

"I sent for you, Gertrude, because Lord Rendover is coming here this afternoon," he began at once.

"Was that all, papa? It seems a very small reason," she replied.

She was rather at a loss what to say, or, perhaps, she would not have answered quite in this way. It was a fortunate answer, however; for it enabled her father at once to make his meaning plain.

"A small reason, my child! It seems to me a very big and momentous one. I mean that he is coming here by agreement, made with me—made with me," he reiterated significantly—"in order to ask you in so many words what he has been asking you for a considerable time by his attentions, to be his wife."

"I wish, papa dear, you had mentioned this to me before you had made the agreement with him."

"Why, my child? What would have been the use of doing that?"

"Because he would have been spared the trouble of coming."

"Spared the trouble of coming! What on earth do you mean? The man *must* speak to you himself on the subject. I am quite prepared to do my part of the duty, though your mother seems entirely to have neglected hers; but Lord Rendover must necessarily propose in person. You surely see that?"

"Yes; but, papa dear, there is no use in Lord Rendover's proposing to me, either in person or in any other way."

"And pray why not?"

"Because I cannot possibly accept him."

"Not accept him! Nonsense. Now, Gertrude, don't be affected. But you had better settle all that with him. You can pretend to say no to him as often as you think proper, provided you say yes to him in the end, as of course you will do. This is all I wanted to say to you. He is coming at four o'clock, and you will be ready to see him. I thought you would like to know beforehand."

"But, my dear father, I assure you I have not the least intention of accepting him. Why therefore should I see him?"

"Then what on earth have you meant by accepting all his attentions these last three months?"

"I am not aware that I have been accepting any attentions from him, in the sense in which you use the word. He has been very attentive to you, and to mamma, and to me, to all of us, in fact, but not to me particularly."

"But it was all meant for you, and you know that well enough."

"I know one thing, papa, and one only, and it is this: that Lord Rendover is no more in love with me than I am with him. Had I ever for one moment suspected that he was, I should have acted quite differently. I had no right to be rude to him, or to refuse politeness from him, particularly when it was paid equally to mamma and to you. But I beg distinctly to say that I have never accepted what is ordinarily meant by attentions from Lord Rendover, and I should never dream of doing so."

"Rubbish, Gertrude! I wonder that a girl of your sense can pretend to make such ridiculous distinctions! Of course you will accept Lord Rendover. There is not a girl in England who would not; and I am at a loss to conceive what you make this scene for, as I cannot think that you do it only in order to annoy me."

"I should think not. I am sure, papa dear, the very last thing in the world I would ever do willingly would be to annoy you."

"Then I can tell you, you will annoy me very much if you do not accept Lord Rendover, and this very day. For there's no sense in keeping the man dangling or waiting. That's all very well for very young or very foolish girls to do to a parcel of boys. But for a girl of your age and dignity to do so to a man in Lord Rendover's position— it is out of the question."

"But, papa, that is precisely why I want to avoid seeing him at all to-day," she urged.

"Nonsense, Gertrude! You *must* see him to-day. I have made the appointment for you, and I expect you to keep it, just as much as if you had made it yourself. Now, no more of this. At four o'clock then. There, go. And I am sure, when the moment comes, you will act in a manner worthy of yourself and of him."

"That I will," she said to herself, when she had left the study and was in the hall, just before going up to her own room.

She had scarcely reached it when there was the postman's knock; and a few minutes later a letter was brought to her by her maid.

"Thank you, Janet," she said; "I will ring when I want you."

The letter was from Chichester Fleetwood, and ran as follows:

"DEAR MISS BLESSINGTON—

"I have been very unfortunate, and for the present am a ruined man. Despite the little encouragement which you have given me, I feel myself bound to tell you this, in order that you may know that no diminution in my admiration and regard for you is the cause of my desisting from a suit which my completely altered circumstances would now make it dishonourable in me to think of urging.

Please to show this letter to nobody. It is the last request I make of you. I wish you every happiness.

"I am, with the greatest respect,

"Yours most sincerely,

"CHICHESTER FLEETWOOD."

She had heard, as most people had, of the big bet that had been made between him and Lord Rendover, and she knew, or could guess, from what Percy Carryngton had told her, and what other people did not know, that Lord Rendover had been the cause of his huge and useless expenditure at Leverstoke. She read the letter over once more and then destroyed it.

"So he has succeeded in ruining the poor fellow, and—as far as I can see—on my account. Oh, why is it not four o'clock? I will try to make matters between them as even as I can."

It was the first time, for very long, that she had felt furiously angry. She looked at her watch — it was half-past two. In an hour and a half the interview was to take place. She only wished it was going to take place this very minute.

Four o'clock came, however, and with it an intimation that Lord Rendover was in the drawing-room. She went down at once, and found him there, and alone. He advanced to meet her, and held out his hand. She gave him hers, but accompanied the action with no other sign of welcome, much less of cordiality. She did not ask him to sit down, neither did she do so herself. Probably she wanted to hurry matters on, and have done with them. He could not fail to remark the discouraging character of her demeanour; but he had himself chosen the moment, and he could not now avoid the question for which it had been purposely selected.

"You perhaps know, Miss Blessington, my motive in seeking this interview with you to-day."

"I do," she said.

"It was in order to declare to you what

I have long felt, and what I have striven to show in every way that I thought and hoped might not be displeasing to you—my earnest desire to make you my wife. I love you, Gertrude——"

"Silence, my lord!" she said. "You have no right to say that to me. You know that you do not as well as I do. But whatever you say, be good enough to give me the only title which I can permit you to use—the one you have always used hitherto."

"Pardon me, if I offended. I will do as you command. But, my dear Miss Blessington——"

"I would rather not hear unnecessary words of familiarity, my lord. If you wish to address me, address me as Miss Blessington."

"I fear I must have done something, unknowingly, to offend you," he said. "If I have, will you not kindly tell me before I say anything more?"

"Do you really wish me to do so, my

lord?" she asked. "If you will take my advice, you will not ask, but me 'will at once bring this interview to an end, and not seek to have any similar one with me."

" But I *must* ask you. I really do wish it."

" Then I will tell you. You *have* offended me. Not *me* personally, not me even merely as woman. You offend me simply as one— I trust of many—whom foul play and underhand conduct and all that is base offends. Others may not know it, but I do. Others may know it, and not have a right to say it. But I know it, and have a right to say it, the moment that you, although debased by such low plots, dare insult me by telling me that you wish to make me your wife !"

" Pray to what do you allude, Miss Blessington ?" he asked, with astonishment.

"You insist upon knowing then ?" she said, her indignation now fairly aroused. " Then I will tell you. I allude to your picking out an honest man for the furtive victim of your envious spite, and devoting

the influence an'd wealth which you possess
and disgrace, to the prosecution of his ruin.
Do you understand me now, and will you
go?" and she pointed to the door, "or must
I speak more plainly still?"

"Upon my word, I have not the faintest
notion of what you mean."

"You lie, my lord, and you know it. You
know that I allude to the mine you sprung
on an unsuspecting man at Leverstoke, to the
trap you set, to the trick you played; trick
worthy of a low blackleg rather than of a
peer of England. I allude to the bet you
made with the same man, with the same
set insidious purpose. I allude—but enough.
Have you not heard sufficient to make you
comprehend that I thoroughly despise you,
and that were I a man, I would horsewhip
you on the spot?"

"I have heard not only enough, Miss
Blessington, but too much," he answered,
moving towards the door. "The girl who
could believe such falsehoods of me is not
fit to be my wife; and I must add that the

girl who could believe thus easily and
rail about them thus unmeasuredly, is
scarcely fit to be a wife at all."

She followed him with a look of silent
scorn as he opened the door and passed out,
and then she sank upon the ottoman with
the exclamation—

"Thank Heaven, that's done!"

No bell had been rung to summon the
servant.   Unushered, Edward Lord Rendover let himself out into the street.

"By ——! she loves Fleetwood, after all,
and that woman at the Underhills' ball was
wrong.   Wont I wing him, though, and be
even with them both?   He shall marry
Jessie; that's what I'll do with him.   She
promised she would marry anybody.   He
shall marry Jessie, and at once, or I'll post
him at Tattersall's on Monday morning as
a defaulter.   By Heaven, I will!   I will
frighten Thornton by letting him know that
those two fellows have broken loose, and
would be much more likely to find him if
he was to live with her than if he remains

alone with me. And I'll send him with my terms to Fleetwood this very afternoon, and they are the only terms I will listen to. He shall marry her straight off, or be posted on Monday to a certainty. And there couldn't be a better way of getting rid of her too at the same time. You've done me a better turn by your insolence, Miss Blessington, than you thought for. By Jove! it's splendid, and I'll do it at once."

He jumped into a Hansom, and hurried off to Park Lane.

CHAPTER III.

BIDDING FAREWELL.

THAT same evening found Gertrude again at her friend Guinivere's, and the following afternoon Carryngton mustered courage to call once more upon Mrs. Morris, though he had been there only the day before. What did it matter? Very likely it would be the last time he should ever call there at all, and Mrs. Morris was the kindest creature in the world, and would think nothing of his going and coming as often as he liked. She probably saw into the state of his feelings—when are good women ever deceived in such matters?—and she would accordingly compassionate and bear with him. He devoutly hoped that he should see Miss

Blessington there. If he did not, he must act without obtaining her advice, and send the answer to Rendover which he had already written and had with him. He would not be able any longer to delay replying to the letter containing the £400 cheque.

The real turning-point of his life had come, and it opened out for him a prospect as dreary and discouraging as could well be conceived. The former turn in his life, seven years ago, had been, though an alluring and hopeful, a deluding and fruitless one. It had been completely wrong, and now he had to turn back, and find a road for himself some other way.

In the very lowest spirits he started for the west. On arriving at his destination, he asked for the lady of the house, was told that she was at home, and was shown into the drawing-room.

He took out of his pocket a copy of Lord Rendover's letter, which he had made, and read it over to himself once more, and then he took out his proposed reply to it, and read that over too. He did not see how he could answer it otherwise. There was a slight delay in anybody's coming. He grew nervous and impatient. He thought he heard the rustle of a dress on the staircase, He put the letters hurriedly back in his pocket. It was Mrs. Grantley Morris who was coming. There was a hand on the handle of the door; the door opened—it was Miss Blessington.

"Oh, how glad I am it is you, and that you are here!" he said at once. "I did want to see you so much, Miss Blessington."

"I am so sorry I was not here yesterday," she said, sweetly. "I would not have gone away, had I not been absolutely obliged. Papa wanted to see me, and therefore I had no choice. I received your note and its enclosure. Here it is." And she drew Lord Rendover's letter to him out of her pocket, and gave it to him.

"You have read it carefully?" he asked.

"Most carefully; and I have also done

what you wished me to do—thought it quietly over."

" I have already answered it," he said.

" But not sent your answer, I hope ?"

" No ; but I should have been obliged to do so, had I failed in seeing you to-day. That was what made me so anxious."

" And do you want to show me your answer ?"

"Certainly I do, and I have brought it with me on purpose. But before I read it to you, there is just one thing that I want to say. It is this. We men, Miss Blessington, are different from you in money matters. As a rule we are less careful, less conscientious if you like. Nearly all men have current debts, rich men just as much as poor men. I am no exception, and there is always a certain number of bills of mine lying unpaid. I say this beforehand, in order that you may understand what I say in this reply, to the cheque alluded to in the letter which you have already read."

"Very well," she said; "I understand. Will you read it me now?"

He read as follows:

"Dear Rendover—

"Your letter so painfully confirms the suspicions I had already begun to entertain of the view which you take of the relations subsisting between us, that I feel myself compelled in honour to bring them to a close. Accordingly, I can no longer accept the allowance which you have hitherto been good enough to make me.

"I do not, however, return the £400 cheque, and for this reason. Without it, I should not be able at once to defray various liabilities to tradesmen, which I can no longer allow to remain unsettled, and which I should never have incurred but for the position which I recently occupied and the expectations which you held out to me at the time of my incurring them. I therefore consider the four hundred pounds as belonging to these tradespeople rather

than to you or to me. Should there be
anything over after I have settled everything, I will pay it in to your credit at the
bank.

　　　" Yours sincerely,
　　　　　" PERCY CARRYNGTON."

"Will it do?" he asked, when he had
finished reading it. "And do you understand it all?"

"I understand it perfectly, Mr. Carryngton, and I have not a single suggestion to
make. It could not be better."

"And I may send it at once, then?"

"At once. · Really, I do not see that you
require my advice or anybody else's. You
have shown in that letter, if you will permit me to say so, so true a sense of honour
united to such soundness of judgment, that
it would be impertinence in anybody like
me to presume to counsel you."

"Don't say that," he pleaded. "If I see
rightly now, it is because you have helped
me so much hitherto. And you quite see

and approve my reasons for making use of the four hundred pounds?"

"Unquestionably. As you say, it belongs to your tradesmen. And what are you going to do now?"

"I am going away," he answered, "and I came to tell you so."

"And with what object? And where are you going to?"

"I propose to myself to go to Nice."

"What to do there?"

"Nothing there, except to use Nice as a base of operations," he answered, with a sort of smile. "It is no use remaining in London or in England at all. The place is too big, and the competition for employment, among such fellows as myself, too keen, for any good to be got by staying here. Of course, all Rendover's influence is gone, and with it, I may be sure, that of a good many other people. Here I should be forgotten, except to be avoided or pitied by the people who once knew me."

" And how would you be better at Nice?" she asked.

"There I could preserve the exterior of a gentleman, and keep myself to the front and well in view. That is absolutely necessary, I assure you, for anybody's advancement. To be shabby, is to be eschewed; to seem poor, is to scare away the assistance of wealth. I have still about a hundred a year of my own, and at Nice that would be enough for the purpose I allude to. I should see scores of my old London acquaintances, as they passed through or visited it; and I could mix among these without provoking their dangerous compassion. Finding that I did not appear absolutely to want anything to do, they would be all the more ready to help me to get it."

"How much more noble, Mr. Carryngton," she said, "you are in practice than in theory. At the present moment you are making a great sacrifice in order to have the satisfaction of feeling that you have demeaned yourself with spirit, dignity, and self-respect. But, though so chivalrous at the instant when immediate decision is required, all belief in the grand and the noble deserts you when you face the future."

There was a tone of mingled admiration and regret in these words. But the former predominated so largely over the latter, that he did not feel himself very severely rebuked. Nevertheless, he replied—

"I am sorry that I should seem to you lacking in faith, but I can act only according to my own poor light. Had it been my lot to have always had such a one as you by my side, it might have been different."

"I have faith in you, however," she said, quickly. "Whenever it comes to a practical matter, I am sure you will act in a manner worthy of yourself. So it does not much matter."

"I hope I shall," he said, a little mournfully; "and the remembrance of you and your nobleness and all your kindness, will be sure to help me. Do not be angry with me," he said, placing his hand upon hers.

" Bear with me ; for I am going. I should not like to go without telling you something. I think it would not be fair either to you or to me, not to let you know it. I almost feel as if you were entitled to the knowledge, and as if it would be a slur upon me, upon my sense and appreciation of what is beautiful and good, if I did not plainly say it. This is no suit I am urging. Any such idea is out of the question. But bear with me passively, my dear Miss Blessington, now that, before we part, I tell you that I have not been so insensible to your worth and your grace as not to love you. I love you with all my heart and all my reverence, and I shall always do so."

He stopped, for manly tears were in his throat. He rose to his feet, and held out his hand.

" Good-bye," he said. " Don't go through Nice without asking for me."

She too rose, and took his hand, but she retained it. She gazed straight and fixedly into his face till the tears that had been only in his voice, trembled into his eyes.

"No, Percy, it cannot be," she said; "I cannot let you go away like this. It would do you no good to go away like this. Better, much better than this, that you should not care for me at all. I know you would not indulge in idle sentiment for sentiment's sake. I feel sure that you love me."

"God knows I do!" he said, solemnly and tremulously.

"Then you must not go away thinking that you are the sport of fortune, and that your fight is with Fate. The man who fancies that Fate is his foe, goes on ever increasing his self-love at the expense of his courage. I will not weaken you, if I can help it, in a future where strength will be so requisite. If you really love me, do not shrink from hearing if, under any circumstances, you would not have loved in vain."

What did she mean? He had at times half hoped that she more than cared for him; that she almost loved, or under more favouring conditions, might have come to love him. Now it seemed as though she not only did not love him, but wished to tell him that she did not and never by any possibility could.

"Do you mean," he asked, "that I must ask you if you love me, in order that I may be forced in after times to look back and see plainly that it was not Fate, but you yourself, who would for ever have made my love a useless aspiration?"

"I do mean that you should ask me that," she said, letting go his hand, which she had kept all this time.

"No—no!" he exclaimed. "I could not bear to hear it. I understand you, and it is enough. I will never accuse Fate, I promise you I never will. I will cherish my love, and accuse only my own acknowledged unworthiness. Good-bye! Good-bye!"

She clutched at his arm.

"Stay, Percy, stay! Whatever right I may have to do as I please with myself, I have no right to sacrifice your future to a form or a blunder.   Do you really—really love me?"

"I do, with all my heart and soul and life?"

"Then—then——" and she paused.

She had raised her arms, and a light had shot up into her eyes, which even to dullest vision could be no other light but one.   He saw it in an instant.

"But you *do* love me?" he exclaimed.

She fell upon his breast.

"Yes, Percy, I do.   How could you ever doubt it?"

CHAPTER IV.

A LOVE MATCH.

THE last leaves of autumn had been shed in the far-away country woodlands; but the sharpness of the clear blue sky and the hard dryness of the road and pavement, unmistakeably attested the genuine advent of winter, even in those north-west parts of London where, though there is abundance of summer foliage, its premature fall prevents it from being of any assistance in defining the separation of the last two seasons of the year.

It is pleasant, that bright brisk freshness of commencing winter, in the wide-stretching, semi-suburban quarter which divides its allegiance between the metropolis and the country; and this morning was the very best sample of this peculiar form of pleasantness. On the main ways, the omnibuses running every five minutes, and now and then a Hansom cab whirling along at redoubled pace and rejoicing in the breadth and freedom of the road, sent out from their wheels a peculiarly sharp sound that almost smacked of frost. The voices of the fruit and vegetable sellers rang more clearly through the air; and ever and anon the scent of violets escaped from the basket of some meek woman, who assured you that they were only twopence a bunch.

But off these main roads there run quiet by-way rows of houses, that usually call themselves terraces; and if you can only get to the further end of one of them, you may have not only quietness and rest for the ear, but now and then a veritable glimpse into real country beyond, of a genuine rural steeple, and of pale white clouds that actually repose, not on roofs, but on the horizon.

If you happen to love such quiet and such glimpses, and must perforce live in a modest way within five miles of Charing Cross, and you happen to find a terrace where all these requisites are •to be had, you cannot refuse to live in it because it is called by such a sentimental name as Ranunculus. It had at first been a matter of objection, and still was a subject of frequent joke and quiet laughter between them. Nevertheless, Mr. and Mrs. Percy Carryngton were living at No. 11, Ranunculus Terrace, N.W.

Gertrude Blessington was married then? Precisely, and to the only man whom she had ever loved. When, four months ago, she had come to the conclusion, upon his so warmly, if hopelessly avowing his love for her, that it was anything but well for him to remain ignorant of her love for him, she had not done so from sheer sentiment, or even a mere impulse of affection. Her reason had been at one with her heart, and she had acted no less conscientiously than bravely and nobly.

She already knew his character thoroughly;
and she had felt quite sure that if, loving
her intensely as he plainly enough did, he
went away to Nice or anywhere else without
being made aware that his love was returned,
any hope of his ever doing anything in this
world useful either to it or to himself would
be gone for ever.   He would never trouble
himself to obtain the advancement of which
he had spoken; he would not even accept
it, she was quite sure, even if it was thrust ▾
upon him, unless it came in an easy, pleasant,
indolent, elegant form, and left him plenty
of leisure to waste his heart and days in
dreaming dreams of her, by distance ideal-
ized and exalted into a supernatural vision.

This at the very best she had felt would be
his lot if, bound by custom and perhaps a
little by instinct, she had allowed him to
say his melancholy good-bye, had held her
peace, and let him go.   But it was not at
all improbable that, bad as this seemed to
her, his future might be even considerably
worse.   Dreaming of dreams is not a very

fruitful occupation, but at any rate it is not
a very degrading one. When, however, it
comes to be mingled with much billiards,
much smoking, cards, damaged reputations,
and English Continental refugees generally,
it may lose a good deal of its harmlessness
and partly assume the colour of what it
works in. And Percy Carryngton, if thus
silently dismissed, might possibly come even
to this.

It would, however, have been very much
harder for her to act as we have seen that
she acted—delicately and dexterously as I
think she did it—had she, by so doing,
been imposing upon him years of unaided
toil, with her only at the end of it and as a
sort of guerdon for his successful labour.
Men may and not unoften do impose such
tasks upon themselves in the hope of such
rewards, and all honour to them for so
doing. But a girl must be very sure of
a man's love before actually consenting to
so arduous an arrangement; and it may be
questioned if any girl would ever feel justi-

fied in herself imposing it. This Gertrude would have been doing, had she, in almost forcing Percy to ask her if she loved him, had no alternative to offer him but that of working in order to win her, or that of giving her up altogether.

Fortunately, however, this was not the case. She had some four hundred a year in her own right. He was quite ignorant of this, but she very soon apprized him of it, plainly declared that if he loved her as he said he did, he must marry her upon it at once, and so permit it and her to aid him in reaching that honourable and useful future which she had fully made up her mind should, in the long run, be his.

Thereupon ensued a scene in which there was not quite that unanimity of sentiment which had prevailed during the one on which we immediately dropped the curtain at the end of the last chapter. Men— Englishmen, at least—are so accustomed to regard themselves as the bread-winners, or at least bread-finders, in some form, that

their ideas of dignity and right revolt
against competency that comes wholly from
a wife. I speak, of course, of the majority;
and, as a rule, I agree with them. Probably
Gertrude Blessington would have likewise
agreed with them; but she regarded theirs
as an exceptional instance, and urged its
exceptional nature. Percy, however, was
very slow to admit a distinction which was
to redound to his own advantage.

"It is impossible, my darling!" he had
said. "You must let me go and work, and
then come back for you. I *will* work now;
here, there, or anywhere, now that I know
for certain that you love me. What will
bring me back to you soonest? I will
carry stones or cobble shoes," he added,
smiling, "or do anything that will most
quickly bring me what I want. But I
cannot—I cannot do what you propose."

"You must, Percy," she answered, resolutely, "or—or—I do not like to say it—but,
in a word, you must do it. You are not as
noble as I imagine you to be, if you refuse."

"Noble, Gertrude! Everybody will say that I am base."

"And does your nobleness depend on what people say of you? Suppose people take an ignoble view of things, how can they be fit judges of what is really noble? There are many points in which public opinion is sound, and strengthens and assists one's own conscience; but there are others in which it is utterly unsound, and our conscience must resist it to the death."

"But my conscience agrees with public opinion on this point."

"You mean your prejudices do. You have lived so entirely amidst this public opinion, that it has sunk into you, and you imagine it to be your own opinion, your conscience in fact. But, Percy, it is nothing of the kind. You have probably never considered the question at all. You have assumed or rather accepted the solution of it, such as you found it about you and ready to hand. And the self-love of sex—the so-

called dignity of man—helps to confirm
you in your prepossessions."

"I am sure I can never rid myself
of it."

"You must," she answered, "or I can
never be your wife; for I should never
think that you really loved me, as long as
you loved this mistaken dignity and this
dreaded public opinion still more than me."

"But what will your father say? And
what could I reply?"

"Now we are coming to it. Let us
forget public opinion, and think only of
what papa would say, though you must see
that papa is only public opinion in a smaller
and more convenient compass."

"He would say that I was a mean-spirited
fellow, that I was an adventurer, that I had
married you for your money, that——"

"Yes, he would say all that, and a great
deal more, I dare say, and in still more
offensive language. I am sure of it."

"Well, my darling, and what could I
reply?"

"What *could* you reply, Percy?" she asked, standing away from him a little, as though waiting for an appropriate answer before she could go near to him again. "I imagined it would be easy."

"I could only reply that it was not true."

"Precisely," she said, going back to him. "And what better reply could you possibly make?"

"Your papa would not think so."

"But that is going back to the old position. It is permitting yourself to be guided in your conduct by what other people think instead of what you yourself think. Now, look here, Percy, I shall have plenty to do to meet the storm which is now sure to burst upon my head. I may tell you *now*," she said, significantly.

(He did not know what she was going to tell him, but he knew what she meant by "now," and he pressed her to his heart and kissed her yet once again).

"I may tell you *now*. Yesterday, Lord

Rendover proposed to me, and of course I refused him."

"Did he?" exclaimed Percy, triumphantly and with glowing eyes, delighted that his victory should be swollen by so high and splendid a prisoner. Lovers cannot help piquing themselves on the discomfiture of the previously rejected, as though they themselves had inflicted the defeat. "Did he? And you refused him at once?"

"Of course," she replied, quietly. "That refusal has already made and will long continue to make my home not particularly agreeable to me."

"I will take you from it at once," burst out the exultant lover, with splendid and spontaneous inconsistency.

"You cannot do that, quite," she answered, with a smile. "But you can materially assist in mitigating by your future conduct a position which your conduct of to-day, sir!"— she said this with beautiful banter—"which your conduct of to-day, sir, will very materially aggravate. Of this last you may be quite sure."

"I suppose so," he said, with very little penitence in his tone.

" I shall have to bear the brunt of double reproaches—reproaches for having first refused so magnificent a person as your cousin, and secondly, for having accepted so wretched a fellow as yourself. Do you understand that?"

There are various ways of manifesting intelligence and expressing consent. But I am bound to say his was the most peculiar way of doing so that can be conceived. It probably can be conceived, however; and therefore I will only say that, having disentangled herself from the consequences of her pretty impertinence, she went on—

"Now, I think the very least that you can do is to help me bear the burthen for which you are mainly responsible. Do you see that too?"

He saw that also, and expressed his seeing it in a manner somewhat similar to his last burst of intelligence.

"The most effectual mode of doing so will be for you to go bravely and tell my father what has occurred, listen to his fury —for furious he will unquestionably be— and then when he has done, assure him that, in spite of all the uncomplimentary language in the world, you have quite made up your mind to marry me, and at present on the strength of what is called my money, and that you will leave it to the future to justify you for what you have done."

"But," objected Percy, "he will simply turn me out of the house, and take good care that I never enter it again, and never see you any more."

"Oh no, he will not. Trust me for that. He will try, I know; but I will take very good care that he does not succeed. If you only prove yourself in earnest, I will be in earnest too. Indeed you must be, Percy— I am speaking quite seriously now—or there

must be an end between us. I tell you I will
marry you at once and from my father's
house, or never. You have no right to ask
me to bear, unaided, years of domestic misery
and parental reproaches."

She very soon found that this was much
the best way of appealing to him. All the
excellent and unanswerable arguments in
the world were not so potent as the simple
picture of her being deserted and handed
over by him, for an indefinite number of
years, to home trouble and unkindness. She
was perhaps a little disappointed that her
lofty appeals to conscience and independence
of judgment should have failed to convince
him, whilst the mere mention of threatened
sorrow to her persuaded him immediately.
Nevertheless, she had the consolation of feeling that, if his reason on its grander side
was a little obtuse, his love for her was very
sensitive on all sides. And this consolation
was no small matter.

As may be conjectured, there were several
interviews of a painful and disagreeable

nature; two especially, in one of which
father and daughter were the personages,
and in the other of which figured father and
would-be son-in-law. Percy had to put up
with some very pretty remarks from the
squire, and more than once was on the
point of losing his patience and temper.
But he was so stubbornly supported, in the
real point at issue, by his brave girl, that
he could afford to tolerate some unreasonable
language on the part of her parent.

Gertrude displayed not firmness alone,
but very considerable powers of management.
She began at once by declaring that she was
going to be Mr. Carryngton's wife, and that
very shortly. Then, said the squire, she
might marry him as best she could, for he
would have nothing to say to it.

But this very small concession by no
means contented her. She took upon herself to point out what a misfortune it would
be for him and for his name if a daughter
of his married against his consent, or even
without his countenance. She did not say

this to him in so many words; but she contrived in various ways to keep it constantly
before his mind, knowing what an influence
it would have upon him. And in a very
short time Mr. Blessington arrived at the
clear recognition of two facts, the first of
which was that, if he refused his consent,
his daughter would marry without it, and
the second, that if she did so, he and his
family would lose greatly in their own
esteem and that of everybody else.

Then it was that poor Mrs. Blessington,
who had been completely set aside and
treated with such indignity, was again not
only permitted but positively invited, by
her testy and bothered husband, to interfere
once more and play the inferior but important part of mediator and concoctor of
compromises.

" The girl *will* marry the fellow," he said.
" That is plain enough. He has got round
her somehow; how, Heaven only knows;
for I see nothing in him of any kind, except
that he knows how to dress himself. He's

a fellow one would never have heard of, if
it hadn't been for Rendover, who picked
him up somewhere, and gave him clothes to
his back, and then found out to his cost
what a fool he had made of himself by
doing so—a base, ungrateful, money-seek-
ing——"

"There—there! my dear George!" Mrs.
Blessington had ventured to say, "I'm sure
he's not all that; and even if he is, it's no
use saying so, now that you've made up
your mind to have him for your son-in-law."

"I've made up my mind because I can't
help it, and because I've never had any
assistance from you, as I had a right to
expect."

"I am sure, my dear George——"

"Well, I don't want to hear anything
more upon that subject; I'm sick of it"
(which simply meant that he was reiterating
an unfounded accusation, and did not wish
to hear it once more proved to be such).
"Manage it among you. I wash my hands
of the whole affair. I will go to the church

and give her away, and then I never wish to hear another word on the subject. They shall never have a shilling from me. Unfortunately her own money is her own money, and there's nothing more to be said. But never a shilling of mine, never a shilling of mine, if I had a million."

This last argument had been freely used by him both to Gertrude and Percy already. The latter had received it in silence—"hypocritical silence," as the poor old squire had called it. But Gertrude had plainly spoken out her mind.

"You say, papa, that the estate will go to my cousin Fred, and I always knew that it would."

"Yes, but I have saved money over and above that, and I tell you that, neither now nor at my death, shall either of you ever see a farthing of it."

"Then I can only say, papa, since you choose to speak to me on the subject, that you will be acting most unjustly."

"Not more unjustly than you are acting

to me and everybody, by marrying a man who cannot keep you."

"It is not necessary that he should keep me, as you know. Fortunately, we have plenty between us."

"Between you! It is all yours. There is no *between* in the case."

"I have already said very often that I regard it as such."

"So does he, apparently," sneered her father. "But if you had as little as he has, you'd have seen he would not have wanted to marry you at all."

"I am happy to think," she replied with dignity, "that he would have wanted. Whether, under such circumstances, it would have been possible for him to do so, is another matter, into which there is no necessity to enter."

"I only wish to God those had been the circumstances," exclaimed her father, with irrepressible annoyance—"that you had not had a sixpence of your own—as girls never ought to have—and then it would have been all right. We should never have heard of the fellow who has turned your head, and made us all miserable."

"I am very sorry," she answered, "you or anybody should be miserable on my account, but I do not feel that I am in any way to blame, or that Percy is either. It is manifestly unjust to impute unworthy motives to a man who has voluntarily abandoned splendid prospects in order to preserve his independence."

"Voluntarily abandoned, and preserve his independence, forsooth!" retorted her father. "Fiddlesticks! He has had to abandon his prospects, as you call them, because a better man than himself was sick of keeping him in idleness."

"I happen to know better than that, papa," she answered.

"Yes, you happen to know everything. You women always do."

He was very rude, was the poor old fellow. But then it must be acknowledged that he was suffering the greatest possible

provocation — the provocation of knowing
that he was utterly in the wrong. Being so
completely right enabled Gertrude, on the
other hand, to preserve perfect moderation
of language.

"I know, and must say it in justice, that
Percy made a voluntary abandonment, because he would not allow Lord Rendover to
drag him down to his own level. And in
justice to myself I will add that it was this
knowledge that decided me finally to marry
him. I am marrying him, and not Lord
Rendover, because I consider him, and not
the other, the real noble man."

"Stuff and nonsense! A parcel of school-
girl's sentiment."

"Then if it be sentiment, papa, please
always treat it as such. I can better bear
from you the imputation of being sentimental than of being interested and
mercenary. We may be a couple of
fools, as you have more than once said
we are; but I .think that is the very
worst that can be said of two people who

marry each other and want nothing from anybody."

"Why, you just said it would be very unjust of me not to give you anything, and now you say you do not want it."

"And I do not want it, and I do not ask for it, and I never said a word to you about it till you mentioned the subject. But for all that, when you do mention it, and when you tell me that you have saved money and that I, your only child, shall never have any of it, because I have married one man instead of another, you are unjust and I tell you so. We do not want the money you speak of; that is, we do not seek for it. But we have a moral right to it, or some of it, and you know that, papa, as well as I do."

"You are a very insolent as well as a very undutiful daughter. But you'll never have a penny from me, either of you; never a penny; and that's all about it."

It was not all about it, unfortunately. Poor Gertrude had to go through fresh but similar scenes, till the day came for her to

be led lovingly away to very different ones.
The engagement was a short one, and they
were married in October. The ceremony
was very simple. The squire was as good
as his word. He gave her away at the
altar, and then he coldly bade them good-
bye and went away. There was no wed-
ding-breakfast, no going back home even.
Gertrude was dressed so as to be ready to
start at once for the Isle of Wight, where
they had a fortnight's honeymoon. They
then returned to London, where they had
come to the conclusion that it would be
best for them to live.

"I should like to live in the country,
Percy," she had said to him during the
period of their engagement and when they
were talking all such matters over; "should
like it just as much as you do. But apart
from other considerations, we could not
afford to do so. We could not take an
unfurnished house, because we could not
furnish it; and one already furnished would
be too dear, much too dear."

"I fear it would, as yet," he answered; "I expect we must come round to lodgings in London after all."

"And not such a bad thing to come round to," she answered, cheerfully. "But there are stronger reasons for our living in town. You must keep up your London connexions, as far as we can, and you must manage to make fresh ones that will be of real, and not mere social use. It is just as you said when you talked of going away to Nice (such nonsense!); you must be in a place where people will not lose sight of you. A good many persons will forget us, in any case, when we live in lodgings; and they are welcome to do. But everybody would forget us if we went away and hid ourselves altogether."

"Always right!" he said, kissing her. "Let us go and look for lodgings at once."

It was a fine September day, the day on which this conversation had taken place; and they trotted off together to look for the lodgings which were to be their first future home. Of course they were to be ideal lodgings—such lodgings as had never been seen before; in a word, lovers' lodgings. They were to belong to a model landlady, who was to be neat, pleasant, conscientious, and never exacting. They were to be in a delightful neighbourhood, where there was no noise, and where there were ever so many trees. They were to be almost in the country, and yet there was to be a cab-stand not far off. They were to look all ways, except to the north; and, indeed, I am not sure that they were not to change their prospect according to the season.

They trotted off, as I said, on this errand, and they had to trot off very often again on the same one, before they found anything that would suit them. At last, after seeing some scores, they happed upon Ranunculus Terrace, at the end of which was a house that looked three ways, having its front towards the terrace opposite, its back towards some other houses, but detached ones with gardens, and only recently completed,

6—2

and its one free side (as being the last house in the terrace) towards the green, open country.

It was not at all what they had begun by looking for at first; but it was very much more than they had now for some time, after a series of disappointments, expected to find. It was not the ideal lovers' lodgings, but they made up their minds that it would make a very good married couple's lodgings, who were forced to begin conjugal life in this fashion, and were determined to make the best of it.

They were to have five rooms in all: two sitting-rooms, one of them with a charming bow-window afront the glorious fields; a bedroom and a dressing-room for themselves, and a tiny but pleasant chamber up above for Janet, who clung obstinately to Gertrude in her new fortunes, and declared that she and no other should be Mrs. Percy Carryngton's maid, come what might.

" But, Janet, we shall not be able to give you, at the very most, more than two-thirds of the wages you have had here at home. We shall be very poor, comparatively, and I cannot at all promise that things will mend."

"I don't care for that, miss. I'll come without wage at all, if it's necessary; but I'm not going to leave you till you tell me that you don't want me any more; and if it came to that, then neither wages nor anything else would be any consequence to me again. That they wouldn't, miss!"

"I am sure, Janet, I am very much touched to hear you say so, and I am quite as much attached to you as you are to me. But then I am bound to think of your interests all the more as you do not seem inclined to think of them at all yourself. And you must think not only of the present; you ought to think of the future. You ought to be saving some of your wages."

"And so I do, miss," answered Janet, honestly; "not much, miss, perhaps, but still something."

"And you will not be able to save anything, then, when your wages are lower
than they are now."

"Never mind that, miss. I'll see the last
of you, wherever it may be."

"It will be in lodgings, Janet, in all pro-
bability, and not in a grand house, with
everything fine and comfortable, as you have
been accustomed to in the places you have
had."

"But there'll be you, miss, and that's all
I want."

"But more than that, Janet," her young
mistress went on, determined to put the
matter in the most discouraging form beforehand, "I shall have to ask you then to do
things that you have never done before. I
shall not be able to afford to keep you only
as my maid; you will have to make yourself useful in other ways. You will——"

"I don't care a bit, miss," interrupted
Janet, resolutely. "I'll do anything you
like, even if it came to cooking; for I do
know something about that too, as I used to

help before I first left home, and I once cooked an entire dinner."

"It will not come to that, Janet," said Gertrude, smiling. "But you may have to do housework, and that sort of thing."

"Then I'll do it, miss; and that and everything else that you may want me to do. For I'm sure there's nothing on earth I wouldn't do for you and for such a gentle-man as Mr. Carryngton. For he's the nicest gentleman I ever saw, miss, and if it isn't taking a liberty, I'm very glad you're going to marry him, that I am, though others do say it's a mad thing. But I see no madness in it, I'm sure, and I never wish for better than to serve you both as long as ever you'll keep me."

Brave, true, sound-hearted Janet. I think that, after Percy's love, this affection and fidelity of her north-country maid was the sweetest thing and greatest bit of consola-tion in Gertrude's present position. Janet meant all she said, and almost found her reward in feeling that she was playing a

part, even though a secondary one, in this
story of romance. Surely, however, romantic
feelings, when they manifest themselves in
such a form and under such conditions,
plainly merit the grand if much-abused
appellation of virtue.

So a room was taken for Janet in the
lodgings at Ranunculus Terrace, and Janet
was one day taken to see it, and she declared
it to be the very sort of room she liked, and
she only wished all the bother was over, and
they were all settled there for good.

Mrs. Blessington had all along hoped
that her husband would give in at last, at
least so far as to furnish a house for them
of some sort; but he showed no signs of
relenting whatever. He would go to church
and give the girl away, he said, but not a
thing more would he do. I verily believe
that the mother, had she herself possessed
the means in any form, would have done it
or tried to do it for them herself; so shocking was to her the idea of her daughter
going into lodgings. But she had no money

under her own control; Gertrude's money
having come to her through a maiden aunt
who had died some years ago, and whom the
squire now went about abusing as an " old
fool who never knew what to do with her
money when she was alive, and who could
only make mischief with it when she died,
by leaving it in the absurd way she did;"
which was, to Gertrude absolutely, when she
came of age.

Even as matters stood, the worthy mother
was for doing by a side-wind what she could
not do directly.

" Why not take a house—a small one—
and furnish part of it with as much as you
can spare at first? And I will manage to
send you some things from Worcestershire
and from here too, which will never be
missed—there are far too many chairs in
both the houses—and by degrees your papa
will come round and be more reasonable,
and people will make you presents,
and——"

" No, no," Gertrude had said; " we cannot

do that. Percy would never hear of it, and I should not like it either. Thanks all the same, my dear mother! We shall be very comfortable, and shall do very well."

"I'm sure I don't see how you'll do very well in nasty common lodgings."

"But they are not nasty and common," pleaded Gertrude.

"Well, lodgings, then; lodgings of any sort. I never thought it would come to that." And poor Mrs. Blessington, overcome by the idea, fairly began crying "Had it been a house, any sort of a house, no matter where or how small! But lodgings!"

Lodgings, however, as we have seen, they were, to which Mr. and Mrs. Percy Carryngton went on their return from the Isle of Wight, Janet having gone on previously to Ranunculus Terrace to make everything ready for them, and there to receive them.

Novels are the modern drama, and should not be without their chorus. That chorus

is the world, and this is what the world said
on the occasion—

" Well! of all the monstrous things that
ever happened, this marriage of Gertrude
Blessington is the most monstrous. It is
downright indecent. To have encouraged
Lord Rendover all through the season, and
then to have thrown him over for that
young fellow at the eleventh hour! The
thing is utterly inexplicable, except that
girls are girls, and nobody can ever tell
what they will do. As for Carryngton, he's
a mere adventurer and has behaved in-
famously. And do you know they're living
in lodgings! And do you know he has not
a penny, and is spending her money as fast
as he can? And poor dear Squire Blessington is broken-hearted, and—well, well!"

And here the chorus shakes its head, and
walks for a time off the scene

CHAPTER V.

HUSBAND AND WIFE.

Very early on in the last chapter, we let it appear that Mr. and Mrs. Percy Carryngton were living at number eleven, Ranunculus Terrace, N.W. But having made the avowal thus bluntly, we were compelled to go back a little and relate how they got there, thus disposing of a courtship, a marriage, and a honeymoon, all in one chapter. Indeed, there may be some who would have better pleased had we lingered longer over that part of our story; but we have yet so much left to tell that we could not afford to dally even amid such pleasant situations.

We have got Percy, his wife, and Janet then in Ranunculus Terrace, and it was—it will be remembered—a bright blue forenoon at the very beginning of winter. They had been there now only a very few days; and to-day perhaps for the first time were they feeling that they had regularly settled down. Breakfast had been finished about an hour ago, and husband and wife were standing— in a loving position, we may be sure—at the window that gave them the delightful prospect of open country. Trees there were none, save where green holly broke the lines of stripped hedgerows, and the fields were naturally looking anything but their best. Still it was the open country, and it sparkled.

"I shall go to pay off my tailor to-day," Percy was saying. "It will take all that is left of the £400 cheque, and will require some more besides; but I will be done with him, and have another when I want one; for he is too expensive."

"You will not want one, I am sure, for a very considerable time. I should think you have got clothes to last you for ever. Never was there such a young swell."

"I have got a fair number, and it is fortunate I have; they will last a long time, if
not quite for ever. I fear I shall look too
great a swell, at first, for the Ranunculus
situation; but I shall tone down to it, as
the things wear out. Meanwhile I can
go without gloves, and brush my hat the
wrong way, in order to look the lodging
part better."

"You will do nothing of the kind, sir!"
she answered. "You will wear your things
as long as ever they are nice, and no longer;
and then you will get fresh ones. I mean
you always to be well-dressed, and set
the Ranunculus territory a good example."

"Very well. On one condition, though,"
said Percy.

"And what is that, pray?"

"That you do precisely the same," he
answered.

"Of course I will. We chose Ranunculus because it gave us this window and a
beautiful view; and as we shall perhaps
still spend a little of our time in looking at

each other, neither has a right ever to be ugly
—indeed anything but exceedingly lovely."

I am afraid they were very proud of each
other; which, by the way, in married life,
is little if any other than a dexterous way
of saying that they were very proud of
themselves.

" But, Gertrude darling, I really do think
I must give up all my clubs."

" You must do nothing of the kind," she
answered. "It would be monstrous; you
have given up one of them already, and you
know I was very willing that you should
do so, for it was a worthless sort of a place,
and never could be of any use to you. But
the other two, Percy, you must not give up."

" I shall never go to either of them."

" Oh yes, you will; I'll take care of that.
I will turn you out into the street—I beg
pardon of Ranunculus; the terrace I mean
to say—I will turn you out into the terrace,
and compel you to go. You do not know
what use they may be to you. If you do
not go to them, and go regularly, people

will lose sight of you altogether; the very thing, as you know, to be avoided."

"But, between them, it will cost me sixteen guineas a year."

"I cannot help that. I know I am right. And then they will be an inducement to you to go into town."

"And spend more money in Hansom cabs."

"Nothing of the kind, sir! You will walk; that is what I meant. It will be an inducement to you to walk into town, and so get the exercise that you require."

"Oh dear!" he exclaimed, stretching out his arms and pretending to be lazy; "I had quite forgotten how to walk till we were engaged."

"Then you must learn how to do so again. But I should have thought you had done so already, during the many pilgrimages we made in search of lodgings."

"And so I did. You know I'm a splendid walker; at least I used to be when I was a merry Swiss boy, and clamb half the hills in the Tyrol."

They spent the rest of the morning together; having a short stroll, by way of
exploration, before luncheon. Immediately
after it, he went into town alone, to pay the
bill of which he had spoken, promising however to look in at both of his clubs, and to
stay at each of them at least a quarter of
an hour. Gertrude said, if he would do
this, he might ride back; but he declared
himself quite capable of walking both ways,
and resolved to break himself in at once to
good habits.

It was the first time since their marriage
that they had been so long apart. He
was away three good hours; and he walked
back home at a rapid pace, anxious to
see her again, and fearing that she would be
beginning to feel lonely. She came to
the door to open it for him; for she was
looking into the dusk for his coming, and
heard his step before she could see his
figure.

"Who do you think has been here? I
have had a visitor already."

"Who was it? Guinivere? Or one of the Underhills?"

"Not Guinivere. One of the Underhills, yes. But which of them?"

"How can I tell? There are so many of them. Who?"

"Your friend, Mrs. Atwell Underhill."

"Already! And was Atwell with her?"

"No, she was alone. She drove up in a brougham—a hired one, but exceedingly grand — and she herself was too magnifi-cent."

"Well, and how did you get on to-gether?" he asked.

"Pretty well. I do not like her, you know, and I never shall. She patronized me a little, but I do not mind that; I was amused. But I do not like her, and that is all about it. On the most lenient construc-tion she is just a vain woman, and nothing else."

"That is about the truth," he said; "but she is Atwell's wife, and he is such a good fellow, and was so kind to me when I was

a boy. Besides, you must make allowances
for her. She had no mother to bring her up,
and she has no children; and having no intellect, what then is she to do? We must be
on as good terms as we can."

And there the conversation ended. The
shutters were closed, the curtains were drawn,
and Janet soon appeared to announce dinner.
This, and all meals indeed, were in the sitting-
room to the back, which, however, was
designated with the presumedly more honourable title of Percy's study, though it could
boast but very few books, and very little
study had been done in it as yet.

"Now shall we go back into the other
room?" said Gertrude, as soon as dinner
was over.

"But I want to smoke, you know. And
must I stay here alone?"

"You shall smoke in the other room, as
long as you are content with your meerschaum. It does not make the room smell
afterwards, as cigars do. I found that out
when we were in the Isle of Wight."

7—2

"Come along then, darling. I intend to confine myself to the meerschaum, and pay my club subscriptions—since you insist upon my keeping them up—out of the money saved by giving up cigars."

Nothing could be nicer than their sitting-room. They could not decide whether it was more delightful with the morning sun on it, or now with the shutters closed, the curtains drawn, the lamp lighted, and themselves sitting side by side near the cheerful crackling blaze; he with one hand in hers, and with the other ever and anon directed to his fragrant pipe.

"But I really think I ought to begin at once to try to add to our income. I am sure I could make something of my recollections of Continental travel, with all its strange adventures, in cities and among the mountains."

"I have no doubt you could, Percy dear; but you must not. There is no necessity for it! I am sure you had much better devote yourself, as we agreed before, to

studying and cultivating yourself, and preparing yourself for acquiring both reputation, and proper money reward in the
future. I should not like you to waste
your time and injure yourself by writing—
printing, of course, I mean—anything pre-
maturely, and before it could possibly be
good, merely in order to add a little more to
our means, which are already quite as much
as we require at present."

"But my reputation would not be injured
beforehand," he pleaded—"supposing that I
ever make one——"

"Which of course you will, sir! That is
quite settled."

"All right! I am glad to hear it," he
answered, laughing. "But this great future
reputation would not be injured by my
doing what I propose. I should write what
I was talking of, for magazines, which do
not require one's own signature. I dare say
it would not be very good, but I would do
my best, and I should get something for it,
and nobody would be any wiser."

"But still you would be spending time in doing it which you might employ in preparing yourself later on to do something much better. It would be quite different if we required it. But we do not, I am sure, Percy dear. I am more than satisfied as we are; are not you?"

"As long as you are, darling, of course I am. It is for you, and to make you more comfortable, that I want to work. For you must remember, Gertrude, that we should not be obliged to spend anything I made. We could put it away until it reached such a sum as would furnish a house for ourselves. That is what I should like."

"And that is what you shall do in time. But let us be quite content with lodgings— I am sure these are delightful—for the present. I am sure it would be more than a pity that, merely for the sake of getting into a house of our own a year or two earlier, you should write what would do neither you nor anybody any good, beyond the mere fact of transferring some money from somebody else's pocket into yours."

How she always counselled nobleness! She found him, however, as obstinate on this occasion as he had been on a former one when they had discussed the same question. The arguments went on for some time; his reasoning growing weaker, but her power of convincing him no stronger. She was a little surprised, but had to be satisfied with his giving in for the moment, even though he still seemed to think that he was right. It did not occur to her, we may be sure, to imagine that Percy was influenced in his own mind by another stronger argument which he did not like to use. It would have looked like it, nevertheless, to mere spectators of the debate. They might, however, have been wrong. Certainly she had no such suspicion.

"Why, Percy," she said, after a short pause, "five hundred a year is a very respectable sum, as long as none of it is thrown away. At first no doubt it sounds rather modest to a young gentleman who had eight hundred a year to spend only on himself."

"And to a young lady," he responded, pressing her hand, and smiling through the tobacco-smoke, "who had an indefinite number of hundreds spent upon her in-directly, and a good big sum, I will be bound, directly. To a young lady with her own horse, and her own maid——"

"Which latter she has still. But listen. With five hundred a year we can have— Ranunculus; such a dinner as you had to-day—(I hope it pleased your lordship)——"

"It was capital; an infinitely better dinner than I ever had at a club, always excepting when one went in for dinner à la Lucullus."

"Moreover, we can have two excellent servants, two clubs by the way, can dress like Solomon and the Queen of Sheba in all their glory; have anything, in fact, and go to the seaside in the autumn for a couple of months."

"Can we?" asked Percy, taking his pipe out of his mouth. "Are you quite sure of that? You are? That's stunning, then." And he placidly resumed his smoking.

"Did you hear anything about Mr. Fleetwood at the club to-day?"

"Oh, I forgot to tell you. I asked ever so many fellows—for there was rather a lot of men there to-day—back from shooting and the Continent, you know—but none of them could tell me anything for certain. Nothing more than what one knew already; that he had gone to utter smash, and was believed to be down at Fleetwood Manse, and living there in perfect solitude."

"What do they mean by utter smash? That he is completely ruined?"

"That's about it, I suppose. He went in, as I told you, for some speculation in the City; and you remember my saying that, on the very night of the Underhills' ball, Grantley Morris told me of it, and said that he was sure Fleetwood would make a big thing by it?"

" Yes, perfectly. And he made a very bad thing of it ?"

"Shocking. And then there were the Leverstoke election expenses, and the petition expenses—the petition was withdrawn at last, for no doubt he could not afford to go on with it—and the bet that he lost to Rendover on the Goodwood."

" Which Rendover insisted on being paid, I suppose ?"

" No doubt. He's not the man to go without being paid, especially by a man whom he evidently hated and feared too. Most fellows seem to think that Rendover got all the bet—forty thousand pounds it was—whilst others fancy that he got only part of it, because Fleetwood had got only part of it to give."

" But if he is living, as they say, at Fleetwood Manse, it must still belong to him, and Rendover could insist upon being paid by its being sold." ·

" But he may have mortgaged it, in order to raise the money."

"In that case, Lord Rendover has been paid?"

"True," answered Percy. "And no doubt he has. Trust him. By Jove! how he was sold! Unfortunately, poor Chichester was sold too. What a pity Rendover did not know that there was no chance of your marrying Fleetwood; and then he would have left him alone."

"And you feel satisfied that it was all done out of jealousy, and fear of my accepting Fleetwood."

"Of course it was. Just as, for the same reason, he wrote me that last letter. I'll never believe it was merely out of annoyance with me for not standing for Leverstoke that he did it."

"No, neither do I. He did it because he had begun to suspect that we were fond of each other; of that I am certain. What a pity he did not suspect it before! for then Mr. Fleetwood might have been spared. Poor fellow! I do feel so grieved about him."

"So do I, Gertrude, and I only wish we

were in a position to do anything for him. But it's out of the question."

"It may not be, some day or other. Try to find out if it is really true that he is living down at Fleetwood Manse, quite alone."

"Yes, I will. But it's difficult to get hold of anything but rumour in such matters as these. I'll try, however."

He had finished his pipe, and had laid it down. He drew his chair as much nearer to hers as was possible considering how near they were before, took her hand in both of his, and said, with a curious smile—

"I was talking about Rendover's annoy-ance with me for refusing to oppose Fleet-wood's election, but there was another reason for his being annoyed with me, which I never mentioned to you."

"What was it? And why did you never tell me?" asked Gertrude, wonderingly, and with eyes of considerable curiosity.

"Because," he answered, smiling yet more, "there are some things which we can tell our wives, Gertrude, which we do not tell them before."

Such a speech as this, we may be certain, excited her curiosity all the more strongly. There is a legitimate field of knowledge, closed to many girls, or at least only half opened, which is entirely disclosed to the married woman; and great is usually her avidity in mastering it, and so becoming wiser, but certainly sadder. Gertrude was no exception to the general rule.

"Tell me all about it," she said, trying to draw her chair also nearer to his, but completely failing, as they were already touching. She succeeded only in knocking them together. "Tell me all about it."

"There is not very much to tell; but, such as it is, I will tell you."

And he went on to describe his one visit to the little cottage between Windsor and Bracknell, and the proposition that was made to him after it.

"How shocking!" exclaimed Gertrude. "Are such things possible? And was she really nice? And was she very pretty?"

"She was very pretty, I assure you; and I think I behaved admirably in the matter, don't you think so?"

"How can you joke and smile about it, Percy?" I am ashamed to say that there was a sort of masculine smirk on Percy's face at the moment. "It is too serious, too terrible, too wicked."

"So it is, my darling! I know that. But we are very wicked sometimes in this world, and men are men."

"They are not men," she answered, indignantly, "when they act like that. They are brutes, savages, and ought to be hunted down."

"When they act like what, my love?"

"In the way Lord Rendover must have acted. You say the poor girl looked awfully miserable; did she not?"

"Yes," answered her husband, "but that might have been in consequence of her own fault more than anything else. I do not see how she can be acquitted altogether."

"We do not know. Perhaps not. But we do know what a bad, clever, unscrupulous, powerful man he is ; and he may have injured her just as he has injured Mr. Fleetwood, and just as he tried to injure you, without its being the fault of either of you."

"That's true. But it would not have been quite so easy to injure her without her consent."

"How do we know? If she had acted differently when, without any collusion on her part, you were entrapped into going down there in order to further his schemes, I should judge her less leniently. But you say she behaved with the most perfect modesty and simplicity all the time."

"Yes, poor little creature! She seemed awfully frightened and nervous, and very anxious that I should go away."

"Then she must have been good, or at least not very bad, it seems to me."

"I remember, when I was going away, she called me back suddenly, as if she had something to say to me of great importance. But when I pressed her to tell me, she would not, and pretended that she really had nothing more to say."

"But did you not press her to tell you, Percy?"

"Yes, I did everything in my power. I pressed her, and pressed her, but it was no use. She stuck to it that there was nothing whatsoever that she wished to talk to me about. So what could I do?"

"And was that all that passed between you?"

"Except that I said that, if ever I could be of any service to her, I should always be most happy. And then I went away."

"And you have never seen or heard of her since?"

"Never a word! How was I likely to hear?"

"You are very strange, you men," said Gertrude, with a sigh of sorrowful wonder.

"You know that she was miserable, and that your own cousin was the cause, or partly the cause, of her misery, and she had made a half sort of appeal to you——"

"Which she immediately withdrew."

"Yes, but she had made it. And it never occurred to you to go back some other time, and see if you could be of any use to her!"

"How could I be of any use to her? Besides, after I saw plainly enough what he had made me go down there for, I had every reason not to go there again. It seems to me I could have done no good, and might have been doing a great deal of mischief."

Their hands remained clasped within each other, but there was a long silence. At last, Gertrude said—

"I wonder if she is there still? At the little cottage, I mean."

"Very likely. He has not the same reason now for trying to get rid of her that he had then. Then he thought he should soon be married to you; and his idea, no doubt, was to get rid of her, and fasten her on to me by the same stroke. The brute!"

"What was her name?"

"I have not the faintest notion. I never heard of her before that visit; and he never alluded to her but once, namely, after that visit, when he at once saw that I was not at all likely to fall in with his scheme."

"And you were quite kind to her, that one evening?"

"Of course I was. I made myself as pleasant as ever I could. There were two hours to be spent, and I made the best of them, both on her account and on my own."

Again there was a short silence.

"May we go some day," asked his wife, . "and see if she is still at the cottage."

"Yes, my darling, if you wish it," he answered.

"I do wish it very much, Percy. I think we ought."

Never was her great loveliness so great as in moments like these, when it was suffused with the bright glow of a frankly uttered sense of right. He pressed her to his heart.

"Then we will go the very first fine day we can."

CHAPTER VI.

PURSUED BY THE PAST.

WHEN Percy was struggling so hard against his wife in favour of the theory that he ought at once to begin to do something which would forthwith bring in money, did not the reader have a suspicion of the real motive which prompted him? It was strange, surely, that he should do so, inasmuch as it had been agreed between them that he should seek for no appointment, no post, private or public, no matter how tempting, that did not leave him his hands free to acquire for himself by degrees that knowledge, skill, and reputation, which she had quite made up her mind should successively be his. He was to be both useful and revered, in the fulness of time, even though beginning married life with only five hundred a year.

"You are only nine-and-twenty," she had said, "and I shall be quite content if you are just beginning to make your mark, and be of real service to people, at forty. There is no hurry. But the intervening years must be spent with a set purpose, and not a desultory one. The opportunity comes to every man who really wants it, but how few are ready for it when it does come! *You* shall be."

To this view he had from the first been quite ready to accede. Indeed it harmonized with his own wishes, was flattering to his energies and his hopes, and would give a grand colour to all that he did in the interval. Nevertheless, he wanted to be already devoting himself in part to the acquisition of the lower rewards of labour, and he over and over again returned to the subject, but each time meeting with so decided a difference of opinion from Gertrude, that it became clear that, if he did it at all, he would have to do it in the face of her disapprobation.

She certainly always had the best of the debate.   But was there no argument which her husband might have used and did not, but which nevertheless was the very argument that was influencing his own mind? And has not the reader already guessed that it was the fact of his having gone security for Atwell Underhill's paying off three thousand five hundred pounds in five years?

If the reader had forgotten it, his memory is no worse than Percy's own had been.   He had become engaged to Gertrude almost in the flash of a second, and in a manner which was not calculated to remind a man of the details of his own or his neighbour's affairs.   But more than this.   For some little time before that important interview which had taken place in Mrs. Grantley Morris's drawing-room, that intended farewell which ended in union for ever, he had been brought to regard himself as a man of no substance whatsoever, as next door to a beggar, or at best with just one hundred a year left him by his father, and arising out

of some very perilous foreign stock. It had
become quite clear to him that he would
have to break with Rendover; and that
once done, there would not be a poorer
gentleman on the London pavement. What
wonder then that, neither at the moment of
his engagement nor, to tell the truth, till
shortly before their marriage, did Atwell
Underhill, and his affairs, and his own
liability connected with them, ever cross his
mind. When they suddenly did so, they
crossed it rather unpleasantly.

But what could be done? He could not
get rid of the liability, and he certainly
could not defray it now. Fortunately,
Gertrude's money, which by virtue of its
being absolutely her own would on marriage
become absolutely his, and therefore subject
to his liabilities, had by his desire, no less
than by that of her father, been settled
strictly on herself, and so removed from the
touch of all such danger. His own foreign
stock had been left as it was, perhaps not
being considered by old Blessington as

deserving of notice, and by Percy himself being regarded as a fund that had better remain available in case of real need.

But this settlement before marriage of Gertrude's money on herself, went very far to calm Percy's fears when it first struck him that he was security for Atwell's repaying that big sum of money to the Insurance Company.

"No man can pay what he has not got," he argued to himself, "and I have no longer got what I had or thought I had when I tried to get poor Atwell out of his scrape. They cannot touch her money; so that's all right. What should I say anything about it for? It will simply bother her. No use tormenting one's wife with such things. But I must see Atwell, and remind him of what, after all, he must himself know to be the case, how thoroughly affairs are altered since I first tried to help him."

Accordingly, he saw Atwell and plainly spoke out his mind.

"But have you really thrown Rendover

overboard altogether?" asked his friend. "Have you broken with him completely?"

"Yes, completely; and sent him and his money to the devil."

"I suppose you know best; but it seems a mad thing to have done. At least it's a desperately bad business for me. Of course I never counted upon your paying it for me, in the long run, I mean. I thought perhaps I might be forced to let you help me in paying it, for a time."

It will be remembered how Godiva, in justifying her extravagancies and self-indulgence, had tried to drive this view home upon him. She failed at first; but it seemed as if she had succeeded in the end, as she invariably did in everything she undertook against her poor, brave, yielding husband.

"Only for a time, Percy, old boy, you understand. Of course I knew I should be sure to pay you off the very first year I was made partner. But I confess I thought you would help me for a short time; and now that you say you can't, I don't know what the deuce I shall do."

"Is there no talk of your being made partner?" asked Carryngton.

"None whatever, at present. I rather think our people have not had a very good year, and perhaps that has some influence on them. And then we are on worse terms with most of them than ever; with my confounded relations, I mean. The way they treat Diva is too monstrous for anything; it would try the patience of a saint. She does her very best to keep matters square; but it's no use, they seem determined to quarrel with her."

Upon this subject Carryngton could of course say nothing. He could only listen and be silent.

"I was quite prepared," he said, reverting to what had been said before, "to be of service to you, in meeting part of the claims of the Company, leaving it to you to repay me when you could."

"Thanks so much, old boy! I know that."

"But now it is quite another matter. I assure you we shall not be anything like so well off as you are, as you may imagine from our intention of not taking a house."

"And, by Jove!" answered Atwell, "if you only knew the trouble *we* have to make ends meet. I am sure I do my very best to be economical, and Diva is carefulness itself; she denies herself heaps of things, I can assure you."

I verily believe she had made him believe this too. She could make him believe anything. If wanting, and saying that she wanted, all sorts of things, and not getting them, was denying herself them, Mrs. Atwell Underhill was certainly self-denial itself.

"But in spite of all this, we can save nothing. In fact, I owe a lot of things, I fear," said Atwell, despondingly.

"The devil you do!" exclaimed Percy. "The first six months are just up, and the day for paying the first three hundred and fifty will be here directly—to say nothing of interest on the insurance. How much will you be able to find when the day comes?"

Atwell looked exceedingly uncomfortable, and began to stutter and to stammer, and to pretend to think, and to calculate. But he knew very well already what all the thinking and calculation in the world could not alter, that he had got absolutely nothing —not a five-pound note—ready, wherewith to pay the first instalment of three hundred and fifty pounds. It came out at last, of course.

"You don't say so!" said Percy, horrified, and feeling in reality not a little angry at the discovery. "But you have eight hundred allowed you by the firm, have you not?"

"Yes, but I thought that, perhaps, you would be able to meet it this first time, or that they would not mind being paid till the first year was up, and then we could pay them seven hundred in a lump."

"But, my good fellow, you may be quite

sure they'll do nothing of the kind. And as for my finding three hundred and fifty pounds by the day we are talking of, it's out of the question."

"Then we must make some other arrangement. Can we not get it, to be going on with? If I were to give up my house or sell my furniture, I should simply be ruining myself and my prospects with the firm, who would guess the reason for my doing so at once."

"Of course they would," answered Percy. "I don't want you to do that."

The rest of their conversation was devoted to devising means for meeting the pressing difficulty. We need not stop to listen to it at present, now that we know the real state of affairs, and understand why it was that Percy was so anxious to be making some money, yet did not tell his wife why he was so. Again he thought to himself it was no use telling her. She could not find the money if he did. Besides, he did not like telling her; the thing was so vexing and humiliating. He and Atwell would devise some scheme between them, and stave off the evil day till the latter should become a partner in the great house of Underhill, Morris, and Underhill, and three thousand five hundred pounds would be a mere trifle to him. Meanwhile, however, by not telling Gertrude about it, he was precluded from trying to put himself into a position to be able to bear his part of the burthen which had been incurred. On the whole, he preferred to give way rather than, as he put it to himself, "to bother her about it."

Of course they had a certain number of visitors, and a certain number of visits to return. These were not very numerous, however, as most people of their acquaintance were, of course, out of town at this time of the year. Besides, had they been in town, it was certain that most of them would not have troubled themselves to call. Although Mr. Blessington had been at the marriage ceremony, there had been, as we know, no breakfast, and it was universally understood that the marriage was utterly disapproved by her family, and indeed by the whole world. People who married so strangely, and then went and lived in a distant and inconvenient suburb, and even then went into lodgings, had no right to be surprised—had they?—if the world of fashion—their own former world, remember —abandoned them. Even the phrase is not fair. The fashionable world had not aban-doned them. They had abandoned the fashionable world. It was their own fault, and they must bear the consequences.

The consequences, it must be owned, did not seem very terrible. They appeared to be very happy. Probably they did not at present want any visitors at all. Some, however, they had; and one of them was always welcome. This was Mrs. Grantley Morris, who was for doing all sorts of things for them, if Gertrude would only have al-lowed her.

" No, no, my dear," was Gertrude's

answer to all her kind offers; "we are very
well, and we want nothing. Always excepting your dear friendship and frequent presence, and that I know we shall have."

"That you will," answered Guinivere,
"come what may."

Mr. and Mrs. Blessington were down in
Worcestershire, where they would spend the
coming Christmas, not this year to be
enlivened by the one presence that had
hitherto made it really Christmas, not only
to the squire's house, but to the whole
country side—the presence of Gertrude.
Her father would most certainly not have
come to see them, even had he been in
London. Mrs. Blessington would have
done so very often, no doubt, indeed too
often; and Mrs. Percy Carryngton must
not be deemed unfilial if she was rather
glad than otherwise that her mother was in
the country. The old lady would only have
come and groaned over her daughter's supposed pitiable plight, have wept over the
lodgings, declaimed against the neighbour-

hood, found fault with the cook, suggested this and urged that, and have introduced an element of trouble and grief where all, without her, was perfect tranquillity and joy.

One of the calls that Gertrude had to return was that of Mrs. Atwell Underhill. She herself wished to make it without Percy, and he thought that it would be the most cordial and friendly thing to do. If they are ever to get on at all, he thought to himself, it will be best brought about by leaving them to themselves once or twice, and seeing how they hit it.

"And you would really—really—rather go alone, darling?"

"Yes, I think so. It would look less as if you took me there, and we can talk together, and I can see better what she has in her and what she really is like. And I will promise to make myself as agreeable as ever I can. And when you come home, I will tell you all about it."

"But are you sure you would not like

me to hire you a brougham?" he asked. " I can soon get you one."

"No, Percy, thanks! Indeed no. It is a lovely day; and I will walk there, and take a cab back. You go down to the club and see what is going on, and be home in good time for dinner."

They kissed and parted. When he returned some three hours later, she came to the door, as usual, to meet him; but he could see by her face that she was excited and had something to tell him, and had been longing for him to return in order that she might do so.

"I never will go there again, Percy," she began. "I wonder how you can like her and care for me to go. She is horrid, and that is the plain truth. But listen: let me tell you all."

He took off his coat and gloves, and went into the room and sat down with her by the fireside.

"I had to wait ten minutes at least before she came in; which was not a very well-bred proceeding, to begin with. However, that is a small matter comparatively. About her appearance, when she did come in, I will say nothing."

"Yes, tell me," said Percy, smiling. "I am sure it is worth describing."

"Well, I will do so, later. Now I really don't think, Percy, I am capable of any small, petty jealousy, am I?"

"No, my darling, I am sure you are not. Besides you have no cause for jealousy, small or great."

"I know I have not. But one woman can offend another without making her jealous. And Mrs. Underhill either commenced at once to try to make me so, or she has no sense of delicacy whatsoever."

"Why, what did she do, or say, or—tell me about it."

"She talked about you in a manner that was disgraceful. To talk to anybody about you—to a woman, at least—in such a manner, would be bad enough; but to talk about you like that to me, your wife—it was atrocious. That is the only word."

" Why, what did she say? Did she abuse me very much?"

"Quite the contrary. She praised you, or thought she praised you, in a style that, if anybody else had been present, I do not think I could have endured. What her object was, was clear enough. And she paraded your photographs, of which she has three or four——"

" A dozen, I dare say," said Percy, laughing.

" And made a display of some things you gave her, in a fashion that, whilst intended evidently as an annoyance to me, was dishonouring only to herself."

"Of course, Gertrude darling. I see her doing it. It's just like her. She never will be any different, and it's no use hoping to change her. But she's Atwell's wife, and we must make the best of it."

" No, no, there is no best to be made of it. You know well enough that I am not in the least jealous about what may have passed between you before we were married."

"But nothing passed, my dear child, I assure you, except what might be published at Charing Cross. It is all her stupid vanity and jealousy of you—that's all. You don't suppose I have not given *cartes de visite* and presents to heaps of people besides her. Only they are not such fools as to make use of them in that idiotic way. I give you my word of honour that I never gave her anything or did anything which Atwell did not know of."

"But that is just what I said, Percy dear, and I thoroughly believe it. As I told you, I am not jealous in the least, and she never could make me so. I should be ashamed of myself if I could. But her trying to make me so, is an insult to me and a dishonour to her sex, and I never will go near her again."

"But nobody was there to see, you say. So what does it matter?" urged Percy, using what argument he could think of.

"It matters all the same in the long run. But wait a little. I have not told you all. We were not alone. There came in another visitor before I left. Who do you think it was?"

"How can I guess? Anybody I know?"

"Yes, some one you know very well. But all in good time. I must not spoil the effect of my story, which is quite dramatic."

Here the indignation on Gertrude's face gave way for the moment to a humorous smile, which broadened more and more. Something very funny seemed to be promised, and Percy redoubled his attention.

"When I had been there about ten minutes, during the whole of which her conversation and behaviour were what I have described, I heard a carriage drive up to the door. She rushed to the window to see who it was. Pretty manners again, to say the least of it."

"Oh, you must not mind that. She does not know any better."

"But she ought to do. However, just see the use she made of it. There can be no doubt that she went to the window to see who it was, and she did see. Having seen, she walked back to her seat, settling herself at the mirror—pretty manners again —as she did so, when the door opened, and the servant introduced—whom do you think?"

"Now, how can I guess? Quick, tell me, you tease."

"Lord Rendover."

Percy's first expression was one of silent surprise. But he very soon burst out laughing, and together they indulged in a fit of regular merriment.

"But see, Percy," said Gertrude, the first to recover gravity, "she knew perfectly well that it was Lord Rendover. She must have seen him. The quiet way in which she walked back to her seat, without saying a word to me about who it was, and her smoothing her hair as she passed the mirror, prove it. She knew that if she had said who it was, I should have asked to have avoided meeting him."

"And what did you do when he came in?"

"I sate perfectly still. He bowed to me, and I acknowledged it as slightly as I possily could, consistently with good manners."

"But why did you not get up and bring your visit to an end?"

"Oh, I was not going to do that; that would have been to let her triumph completely. She had suppressed the fact that it was he who had come to call, and had allowed him to be admitted without a word to me, on purpose to disconcert me. You do not suppose that I allowed myself to be disconcerted? Going away at once would have proved me to be so, for I had not been there more than a quarter of an hour at most. I stayed another five minutes or so, and then I left."

"And what happened during those five minutes?"

"Really it is not easy to describe it. She

conducted herself in a way that must be seen to be appreciated."

"I think I know it," said Percy, "just as well as if I had seen it."

"I dare say you do, sir, because you have seen her do it pretty often, perhaps. I have seen you together twice, you know."

"When?" asked Percy, laughing.

"At the Pall Mall theatre once; and the other time at the Underhills' ball. And certainly on the latter occasion you would have given anybody the notion that—well, you know what I mean."

"It's a way she has got," he remarked, still smiling.

"But that was nothing to the way she behaved with Rendover to-day."

"Perhaps he encouraged and helped her more than I did?" suggested Percy, with the roguish twinkle in his eye that showed how infinitely amused he was with the whole story, and how thoroughly true he felt his wife's narrative and description to be.

"Exactly," she replied. "That is pre-

cisely what happened.   They both began at
once playing the same unblushing game, for
no other end that I can see except in order
to try to mortify me."

"I very much doubt if that end would
completely satisfy Rendover."

"You don't mean that !" said Gertrude,
horrified.

"Yes, I do.   But I think she's more than
a match for him."

"At any rate, she is no acquaintance for
me, and I will not know her.   It is the
last time I shall enter Jessamine Lodge."

"They are sure to ask us to dinner soon,"
said Percy, teasing her.

"Then we will not go.   At least I will
not."

"May I go alone?" he asked.

"No, sir, you will not.   But do you
know, I got one piece of information before
I left—which I did with great grace, I
assure you——"

"I have not the slightest doubt of it."

"A piece of information that was worth

having. He told her that he was going down into Suffolk to-morrow."

" Well? I don't quite see the value of the news."

She put her arms round his neck, and looked into his face.

"Do you not? Can you not guess? You are the worst guesser I ever saw. Do you not think it is time to go down to the little cottage to see if that poor girl be there still? He is sure not to be there if he is going into Suffolk; and if the day be fine, may we have a real holiday, and go and see if we can find her and can do anything for her?"

" With all my heart, love."

And so it was settled.

CHAPTER VII.

IT was a lovely December day, blue, and still, and sparkling, and Mr. and Mrs. Percy Carryngton left London by train for Windsor about eleven o'clock. It was the first entire holiday they had taken since they had settled down at Ranunculus Terrace, and since Percy had been supposed to spend all his mornings in close study.

It was delightful enough to them to tear along in the train, leaving the big town behind and to get into the bright crisp country. They had a carriage to themselves by the intervention of an acute and considerate guard who at once took them for what they were—who on earth could

have mistaken them for anything else?—
and who closed the door upon them with
the smothered remark to Percy—

"I'll try not to let anybody else in, sir."

"All right," answered Percy, slipping the
merited sixpence into the furtively respond-
ing palm.

"It's very wrong of you to give anything to the guards, Percy; it only demora-
lizes them, besides throwing away your
money."

"We should not have the carriage to ourselves, if I did not."

"It's wrong, all the same," she said,
much less gravely. "But it is very nice
being alone, nevertheless."

They found it so even in the railway;
but when once they had exchanged it for an
open carriage, and were out of Windsor, and
were driving along the road between the
stripped forest on either hand, their delight
knew no bounds. They were like a couple
of children. Their spirits waxed higher and
higher as the sun did. It was midday;

and as it was now just about the winter
equinox, the heat and sunlight were at their
climax.   Despite the nature of their errand,
thoughts not serious but the most trivial
and laughable thrust themselves upon their
conversation.   They made many not unkind
jokes at the expense of Ranunculus Terrace,
some of whose denizens had thought it their
duty to call upon the young couple.   Percy
and wife had replied to these civilities as
best they could; letting it be seen, however,
that poverty cannot make people equal, when
education and sentiment already stand in
the way to make them unequal.

The ladies of Ranunculus took these hints
with that practical good sense which, whatever superficial people may say to the contrary, is far more the property of women
than of men.   Had Mrs. Percy Carryngton
really been no better than themselves, they
would have been indignant enough at her
supposing that she was.   But seeing clearly
enough that she was infinitely superior,
they frankly acknowledged it, and said that

it was not to be expected the handsome young couple should visit in Ranunculus Terrace. But the husbands were not so tolerant or so sensible. They conceived that British trade had received a most decided insult in their important persons; they vowed deadly war against an insolent aristocracy; and I have no doubt that Mr. and Mrs. Percy Carryngton's conduct influenced the Ranunculus votes at the next election to a very considerable degree.

There was always a good deal of fun, in idle playful moments, to be got out of this subject, and to-day they found fresh jokes to crack upon it. But when Percy said that he thought they were approaching the lane where he must tell the driver to turn off, they grew more steady and serious. In a very short time they would be at the cottage.

"Yes, to the right," said Percy, directing the driver.

"I wonder if she will be there. How long ago is it since you saw her?"

"More than six months. It was either

at the end of May or at the beginning of June, I cannot tell exactly."

"Do you remember her? And should you know her again?"

"Oh yes, perfectly. See, that's the cottage, in there."

"What a pretty little place! It would just do for *us*."

"If you had seen it when I did, with all the trees in full leaf, you would have thought it lovely, I am sure. Shall I go alone, at first?"

"Yes, you had better; for she knows you already, and I should only frighten her, perhaps, unless you prepared her."

"And what shall I say, if she is there?" he asked.

"That you want to bring your wife, if she will let you. Say that."

He went, leaving her in the carriage at the garden-gate. How well he remembered seeing the poor pretty creature, whom he had now come to seek, appearing in the doorway, and being startled into pausing when she beheld him at the foot of the steps! How well he remembered the chairs under the walnut trees, and the tea they had together, and all her nervousness, and simplicity, and sweetness! How plainly he could recall the very tone of her voice, as she had uttered his name in calling him back, and the anxiety in her face that he should go, when, in spite of thus recalling him, she had retired resolutely from her original intention, and assured him most positively that she really had nothing to say to him! His conscience smote him as he thought of all this, and how he had never again tried to see her and serve her. Yes, Gertrude was right. He ought to have come. He hoped sincerely he should find her now.

In about ten minutes, Gertrude saw him coming across the garden, and she was already preparing to get free of the warm travelling-rug which was wrapped round her, in order to be ready to get down, when looking again she saw him, now that he was nearer, shaking his head disappointedly. He had reached the carriage.

"She's not there, darling, I'm sorry to say, and I cannot learn in any way where she is. I'll tell you as much as I heard, as we drive along," he said, getting into the carriage. "For it's no use your getting down, and the sooner we start, the more sun we shall have to go home by. . . . Back to the station!"

The driver turned, and drove away.

"Whom did you see?" asked Gertrude.

"Only an old woman; not very old; middle-aged, perhaps."

"Did she know the girl at all?"

"Yes, and spoke of her as Miss Jessie. That was her Christian name, no doubt. She said she was cook when Jessie was there, and now she was taking care of the house for a gentleman; but she did not intend to stay, it was so lonely now, with nobody there."

"I should think so. And when did she say the girl left?"

"About the beginning of August, she made out."

"Nearly five months ago. But had she no idea where she has gone to?"

"Not the least, she said. The other servant that used to be there had told her that Miss Jessie was going away to be married. But she did not believe a word of that. Only she had gone, and the other servant had gone, and she knew nothing more, except that she was going away too, and that very soon; for it was too lonely, and she would not stay for all the money in Windsor."

"And that was absolutely all you could get out of her?"

"Absolutely all. We are no wiser for our journey."

"But, Percy, do you believe that she went away to be married?"

"Of course not, my dear. Married! Who would marry her?"

"True; who would? What did it mean then?"

"It means nothing very consoling, probably," he answered. "Don't let us talk of it. Poor creature! I'm very sorry for her."

"Oh, I wish we could find her!" exclaimed Gertrude, miserably.

"Perhaps it is but a very poor comfort to think that she is not peculiar; but there are hundreds, thousands, just like her."

"Do you think so, Percy?"

"I know it. Thousands—tens of thousands."

"But not unhappy, and pretty, and shrinking, and timid, as you say she was."

"Well, no, perhaps not. But what is the use of thinking about it? The woman could tell me nothing; not even where the other servant had gone to, or where she came from, or where her people lived, or anything. We must give it up."

"But I do so much want to find her, Percy. I cannot help thinking that she is more or less good, and that we could do something for her if we could only find her.

Oh, I wish we knew where she was! And you really do not believe she is married?"

"The most improbable thing in the world," he answered.

And then they both were silent, with their hands pressed together under the rug, alike influenced by that quiet melancholy which is born of disappointment, and was ministered to by the deepening solemnity of the still winter afternoon, from which the sunlight was being drawn away into the pale saffron clouds.

"And do men feel no remorse for such things?" Gertrude asked her husband, when at length she broke the silence.

"I fear not," he answered. "Not usually, at least. The men who are horrified at such things are commonly the men who would not do them. And then, when a man has perpetrated some great wrong, he directs his attention more to shielding himself from its evil consequences than to ward them off from his victim."

"And you really think that Lord

Rendover was not made at all unhappy by her unhappiness, nor his peace of mind disturbed by her trouble?"

"Not in the least. His peace of mind may have been just a little disturbed; but if it was, it was only out of his anxiety to get rid of her before marrying you. And it looks as though he had succeeded in the first object, however much he has failed in the latter. But, perhaps, after all, he has merely moved her somewhere else, in pursuance of some fresh plan."

"Probably," said Gertrude, mournfully. Her tender heart was wounded to the core, thinking of the poor girl's doom. "Oh, how I do wish that we could find her, and set it all right!"

And was Percy correct in supposing that Lord Rendover was as incapable of feeling remorse after a wrong, as of entertaining a scruple before committing it? I fear he was. But there is a feeling which, whilst having little or nothing in common with remorse, is for the minds that are proof against this last, probably no less terrible and tormenting. It is the fear of being found out and punished.

Lord Rendover had been so accustomed, all his life, to sin, yet not to suffer, to injure, yet never to have to make amends, to inflict wrongs, and reap the immediate profit of inflicting them, and then to forget all about it, that the very first check he met with in such a career was sure to have a remarkable effect upon his mind. He had no moral sense, no care for the consequences of his actions save as they might affect himself. But he had every other sort of sense in abundance; and the moment that he failed, completely failed, in some pet scheme for which he had been earnestly plotting, he became exceedingly sensitive to the fact that he was not invincible. Hitherto he had always succeeded. Now, at last, he had failed. Success evidently was not his vassal. He could no longer comfort himself, in all his nefarious designs, with confidence. He saw that it was necessary to be cautious; and caution, to such a one, is uncommonly like fear.

When, immediately after Miss Blessington's scornful rejection of him, he, in common with the rest of the world, heard that she was going to marry Percy, he could scarcely credit his ears. It is true that he had all along suspected that his young cousin had a tender feeling for her; but he had fully counted upon the other advantages which he held out to Percy far more than counterbalancing so incipient and indefinite an inclination. When Mrs. Atwell Underhill had opened his eyes, at the Underhill ball, not only to Percy's still subsisting, and, indeed, increased tenderness for Gertrude, but also to Gertrude's positive inclination for him, he was mightily astonished. Any danger, however, from such a mutual feeling he fully calculated upon dissipating by his note to Percy; which scarcely left open to the latter any course but the one that he had taken—viz., that of resigning the annual allowance from Rendover.

So that when, in spite of all these pre-
cautions and subtle designs, the upshot of it
was that Percy did marry Gertrude Blessington, Lord Rendover's faith in himself
and in his immunity from failure, received
an enormous shock, for which even other
successes at the same moment did not avail
to compensate him. He began to think
more cautiously and even nervously of
other designs whose fruits he had reaped
or was reaping, but whose ulterior results
had perhaps not yet fully worked themselves out.

The chief cause of his anxiety was the
present freedom of the two burglars, whose
bold escape from confinement, it will be
remembered, he had read in a paragraph in
the paper, the very day that we last saw
him go down to the cottage and extort from
his bewildered prisoner there a promise to
marry anybody on earth. All efforts on the
part of the police to recapture the escaped
convicts had been vain, and Lord Rendover
knew that they had been such. Bully Bill

and Sam Slaughterous were at large, and
they had every reason to owe a lasting
grudge to a man who had assisted in their
conviction, and assisted in it, as they and he
well knew, by absolute perjury. They might
not be able to find their former comrade
Abraham under his excellent disguise of
Richard Thornton; but all the world knew
where Lord Rendover was, and Bully Bill
and Sam Slaughterous were not excluded
from the knowledge. They might still have
no suspicion as to who was the gentleman
for whom, at the instigation of Abraham,
they had taken share in the Dipleydale abduction; but they had understood quite
enough at the trial for burglary to be aware
that Abraham's evidence, if unsupported,
would not have been sufficient to convict
them, and that the conviction for that crime
was therefore largely due to Lord Rendover,
and to Lord Rendover's having sworn falsely
about Samuel Speke's mask falling off whilst
the latter was holding him down in bed.
This would be quite enough to provoke

their vindictiveness, even supposing that they were still completely in the dark as to his share in the November night's dark work, and in their arrest early the following morning at the railway station.

But what security had he that they were completely in the dark upon this question; or, if they were, that they would always or long remain so? Abraham was under his own roof, and was probably beyond the reach of their discovery by his new and respectable position, and by his wonderful red wig; nor had he any reason to fear that his servant would betray him in a matter where betrayal would involve himself. The law was quite ignorant of the Dipleydale abduction. No reward or pardon was, as had been the case in the burglary, offered to anybody who would give queen's evidence; and therefore Thornton could gain nothing by turning informer.

But Jessie still lived, and the ruffians who had smothered her screams and carried her off for him might possibly be thrown across her path—and then? Who could tell? Percy had married Gertrude Blessington, and both Jessie and Bully Bill and Sam Slaughterous might yet be avenged upon their common enemy!

There was a time when he would have laughed such notions to scorn; the time when to wish and to succeed were one, when failure never came within either his ken or his experience, when men and women were merely supple instruments, and Edward Lord Rendover used them at his pleasure, compassing his ends with unerring certainty. But now!

He had been balked once—balked signally—and in the teeth of odds which he had regarded as enormously in his favour. In spite of his rank, his wealth, his cunning, his unscrupulousness; in spite of the squire's favour and influence; in spite of Percy's dependent position; in spite of the encouraging opinion of the world; in spite of all, he had been thoroughly and ignominiously beaten. He was no longer invincible, even in his own eyes. His prestige with himself had gone.

But to lose confidence is to lose nerve; and to lose nerve is to lose coolness. Now, nothing is so much required for the successful prosecution of scoundrelly designs as coolness. Hitherto, Lord Rendover had been probably as cool-headed as any man in Europe; and though comparatively so still, he was not altogether in this respect his former self. Time was when, even had it been possible for him to miss his end, it would have been quite impossible for him to have omitted any conceivable steps or to have made any avoidable blunder in the aiming at it. Now, in this his altered and somewhat heated and nervous frame of mind, it was quite possible that he should even commit some serious blunder or be guilty of some very stupid omission.

He had long ago changed his original intention, made on first reading the unpleasant newspaper paragraph, and had informed Thornton of the escape of his former associates. The poor creature was thrown into unutterable fear, and his alarm was comical to see. For a time, it almost made Rendover feel himself again, just as the sight of a dying man will make an invalid for the moment imagine himself strong. Thornton's pitiable inferiority, whilst bringing home to his master his own vast superiority, at the same time made Rendover feel himself still more superior than he really was, and showed him how necessary, with so wretched subaltern for an accomplice, all the superiority he could muster, would be to him.

But superiority in such matters always shows itself in action. One of the active means taken by Lord Rendover was to do what he had once done, many years before, for sheer amusement—viz., to make a round at night, in the company of a police inspector, of the thieves' and burglars' dens in the metropolis. The inspector was only too grateful to Rendover for thus offering to assist him in his duty of trying to discover the escaped convicts, and too ready to gratify a whim common enough with men, that of going, under proper protection, through the haunts of our criminal population.

The expedition, utterly fruitless on the first occasion, was more than two or three times repeated; and twice Rendover was accompanied by his servant Thornton. Both of them, we may be sure, made the very most of their opportunities, feeling how very much more their minds would be at ease, if these runaway gaol-birds could only again be entrapped. But their journeys and their scrutiny were in vain. The police had been utterly baffled; and these supplementary amateur efforts to aid them, ended by being just as barren of result.

This additional failure only increased Rendover's anxiety. Men who could thus baffle so well organized a system of discovery as that existing in London, and indeed throughout the country, were not men to be despised. He tried to forget all about it; but he was too sensible a man, too much alive to the common results of letting things take their course, to succeed in throwing the matter off his mind in any such fashion. He could not forget it; it haunted him constantly; he always felt anxious; and in weaker moments, he felt even alarmed.

"There is nothing else that I can suggest, Thornton, except your going down, every now and then, to the neighbourhood of Fleetwood Manse, and seeing that everything goes on quietly and regularly there, and that he remains on the spot. As long as everything continues there to be just as it is now, I don't see that there is very much to be anxious about."

But for all his words and his attempted bravado to Thornton, Lord Rendover's anxiety increased rather than lessened. He was vexed with himself to note that, whenever he found himself, either at a railway station, or in the street, or elsewhere, amid or near to a crowd of "roughs," he could not rid himself of the vision of two faces which once confronted him from the felon's dock, whilst he stood up as a witness, and after swearing to tell the whole truth and nothing but the truth, swore falsely against them, as both he and they well knew.

Nor was this the worst. Even his sleep was not sacred from such imaginary but tormenting visitors. The sound of a swollen torrent would rush through his dreams. A face bathed in tears would press slowly upon his slumber; and then he would wake, with his breath all stayed, fancying that a terrible grip was on his throat, such as he had felt when the burglar had held him bound to the bed. Gasping, he would arise; and no mock laughter could dissipate the remembrance of such hideous nightmares.

CHAPTER VIII.

AN IMPORTANT DISCOVERY.

EVERYBODY knows that simple means constantly succeed in baffling very intricate ones. Detectives were looking out for Samuel Speke and William Stebbins in all the populous towns and districts in the land, whilst they were helping to gather in the goodly harvest in one of the most thinly populated parts of the west of England.

This of course was in the month of September; now a considerable time back. But even when all the yellow corn was gathered in, there was still abundance of agricultural labour for them to do; and as long as there was, they remained in the same spot. They were considered good workmen by their employers, and decent fellows enough by their fellow-labourers. They had changed their surnames, and some of their habits, determined to try and start afresh in life if they only could. They lodged in separate cottages, though they usually contrived to get set to work upon the same jobs; and on Sundays and of an evening in the week days they were always much together. Still they were on familiar terms with all their neighbours, who never for an instant suspected their past.

But when, as winter advanced, and work grew more scarce, and there was not only less to do but less to be got for doing it, the old spirit, exorcised for a while by steady toil and the yet fresh recollection of the drawbacks of prison confinement, began anew to stir within them. They were compelled to be idle; and when they were idle they naturally fell into the habit of talking over their old ways and experiences. The further the winter advanced, the more time had they upon their hands; and the more time they had upon their hands, the more their former life became the topic of their talk together. Time too was effacing the wholesome memory of hard gaol discipline; the penalty was being forgotten, at the same time that the deeds for which the penalty had been inflicted were being brought up more vividly before their imagination. A short period back, it was the prison that was so awful. Now, it was the night attempt that had been so "jolly."

And then as the days became shorter and shorter, the old spirit of adventure grew apace with the growth of opportunity. They allowed to themselves, and to each other, that it was just possible they might "try again" some day. The idea had entered in once more. It would have been strange if in such minds it had not ended in growing into action.

Of course they often talked over both their capture and their subsequent trial, and they invariably returned to what appeared to them the salient features of both. Abra-

ham—Abram, as they called him—and Lord
Rendover were frequently in their mouths.
For the latter, however, their predominant
feeling was fear; for Abraham it was
one of unmitigated hatred and vindictiveness.

" I'd willingly go and have another nine
months o' quod, bad as it is," said Stebbins,
"just to have that little brute Abe at the
length o' my arm. You'll never convince
me, Sam, say what you may, that it wasn't
he who laid the trap for us, after the Dipleydale affair, by which as how we was nabbed
the morning after at the station."

"Maybe he did," said Speke. "I don't
say as I'm sure you're wrong; only I see
difficulties where you don't. It's a deal
more likely it was all done by the chap for
whom we carried off the girl."

" True enough, Sam; but then Abram
must have set him on to that, or how could
he ha' knowed anything about it?"

" Then they did it between 'em."

"Why, o' course they did; but that's

just my idee, and always has been. A pretty pair of fools we was, to help to carry off that girl, and never know a bit for whom we was doing it!"

"Abram did us there completely."

"I should think he did—as he always did us. If I only had him," said Stebbins, doubling his enormous fist—"if I only had him within reach o' this, I'd *do* him for good and all."

"I'd a deal sooner know," said the other, "who the chap was for whom we did that bit of abduction. He'd be worth something, he would. How we could squeeze him! And it 'd be worth while squeezing him, if we could only get hold of him, in these times when there's barely aught to do all round."

"Ay, but we're not likely to find him without finding Abram first. We might get to know then. No, next to giving Master Abram a taste o' my fist, I'd next best like to have just five minutes' private conversation with Lord Rendover."

"It 'd be the worst five minutes' conversation you ever had, Bill. You'd be in quod again, within five more."

" I know that, hard enough. But I mean if I could meet him without any danger to either on us! I'd pay him off for swearing agin us as he did. Why did he perjure hisself? say I. If he'd only told the truth straight up, I shouldn't ha' minded. And if he'd only done that, we shouldn't ha' been convicted at all. Why did he perjure hisself about that mask? That's what I want to know. Why?"

When Bully Bill got upon this point, it was impossible to draw him off. He had a monomania upon the subject of the mask. He attributed their being found guilty to this piece of perjury, and he was probably right enough in doing so. He therefore attributed their misfortunes, after Abram, to Lord Rendover's hard swearing.

But if he and his comrade had reason to feel so strong a grudge against his lordship, they had also a much stronger terror of him. They regarded him as the type, almost the very impersonation of that awful thing, regularly constituted and wealthy society, which had been their enemy and whose enemy they had been, as far back as ever they could remember. Had either of them met Abram, they would probably have wrung his neck. Had both of them met Lord Rendover, they would probably have run for their lives.

By the time January had come, they had been so sorely tried by want of regular occupation, and by the temptations to return to their old life which, as above described, enforced idleness only strengthened, that they had fully made up their minds to try their hands at another burglary somewhere. But they were not as well prepared for the attempt as they used regularly to be in the old days. Neither would it do for them to go about seeking to provide themselves with the more scientific apparatus of the cracksman's art. They had most carefully avoided communications with any of their former comrades. They agreed in thinking that their best hope of eluding the police lay in keeping altogether aloof from the class of whose movements the police usually kept themselves pretty accurately informed.

But whilst this determination added to their safety, and was, indeed, perhaps the exclusive cause of it, at the same time it disabled them from undertaking or thinking of undertaking any housebreaking in which great skill and perfect instruments would be required.

They agreed further in deciding that nothing must be done by them anywhere in the neighbourhood of the place where they had now been working for some months, and where they still occasionally, even in these winter months, contrived to get employment. Their movements would necessarily be better known, and so render them more liable to detection.

But there was a stronger motive still, and Samuel laid very great stress upon it, to the complete convincing of his comrade.

" Better leave these parts to fall back on between whiles. Don't you see that, Bill? It's not a bad sort of a neighbourhood, if it weren't for bad times i' winter, and I'd as lief be here in haytime and harvest time as anywheres. You see there's no nabbing of us here, for there's none as suspects us."

" Just so," said Bill; " and there's nothing queer in our going off i' winter, where there's never a thing to do, and we could allus come back as was agreeable. And they're not a bad sort either about; and the ' Three Horse Shoes ' is as cosy a bit of an inn as ever any cove lapped his swizzle in."

But if they were to spare the country in which they now were, where were they to direct their noble efforts? They proposed all sorts of schemes, and wrangled over them in their friendly rough way till February was upon them. Then it was, and not till then, that they hit upon a scheme which completely commanded the approbation of both, the origination of which each claimed, but neither would yield to the other. Perhaps the credit was common. Certainly the consent was. The notion, whosesoever it was, delighted them both exceedingly.

It was nothing more or less than to have another try at Fleetwood Manse. They had made a very decent thing by the last attempt, even though Abraham's treachery had got them into such difficulty on account of it. This time, however, no third person should be engaged. They would have no accomplice, and they knew that they could thoroughly trust each other.

The place itself thoroughly satisfied the two requirements above described. It was eighty or ninety miles from their present place of abode, had no special communication of any kind with it, yet could be easily arrived at on foot and by byeways from the main road. In the second place, it could be entered, unless it had been materially altered, by the application of the very simplest means; means that could be concocted by either of them in half a day.

"Now that we know th' inside and all about them staircases, where's the difficulty?" asked Sam. "We'd get in at that window that Abram opened for us downstairs——"

"I' the dining-room, you mean?"

"I dare say it *is* the dining-room. But I mean the window by which me and you both went in and went out."

"Ay, ay, Sam, I'm with you."

"And then you know we'd get into t' hall and go up the big staircase, not up that little roundabout 'un."

"No, no,—no more o' that little poor thing. It tweaked and made no end of a row. And it led into that big room full of books, and I don't want no more o' *them*. I didn't like all them books at all; they looked uncanny like."

"So they did, Bill. We'll ha' no more o' them. We'll go up the big staircase and into that room out o' which you said you looked out on to t' staircase with Abram, while I held the gent down in bed, and when you got such a sight o' valeyables."

Much more and very long conversation had they to the same effect, before starting finally to carry their plan into execution. It was the middle of February—" Valentine's Day, and better's the luck," as Bill remarked—that they set off, saying that " they were going in search of work, and would like enough be back by the mowing time, and before if they did not find what they wanted."

It took them a week to go and to reconnoitre, and to make up their minds that their plan was a good one, and might be carried out at once without any further delay. They had, however, to wait another couple of days before having a favourable night for the attempt. On the twenty-third, about half past one, they found themselves on the old spot, outside the window which Abraham had opened for them from inside, and through which they had previously entered. Now, they would have to open it for them-

selves. But if everything within was as
little altered as was everything without,
they knew they would have very little difficulty in doing this. The only change that
they noticed about the place was that the
scaffolding up which Abraham had climbed
was no longer there, nor was there indeed
any scaffolding visible about any part of
the house.

Their attempt opened with singular
success. Both window and window-shutter
yielded most kindly to their skill, and they
had never once been interrupted by the
slightest sound of any kind. Before
two o'clock they were standing within the
house, on the very spot where they had
stood and taken off their boots and put on
their masks fifteen months ago.

They had made themselves masks,
and they put them on now. But it was
quite understood between them that they
were not to use personal violence, unless it
became absolutely necessary in self-defence,
and to enable them to escape should there

be any alarm given and any attempt made at seizing them. They had had quite enough experience of violence and its effects. They were to carry off what was worth having; but the moment they found that their presence was known, they were to run for it at once. The masks, however, were an additional safeguard, and they put them on.

Then they took off their boots and listened. The stillness was complete. The door which led from the room they had entered, into the big hall, was open, and they peeped cautiously into it. It was huge and bare, and perfectly still. They crept noiselessly into it. There, at its further end, was the main staircase. They were standing at the foot of it. They looked up at the gallery which ran round at the top of it. Still there was not a breath, not a sound of any kind.

They commenced cautiously ascending the staircase. It was very different from the little spiral one up which they had once crept; and which, with all their care, had creaked horribly all the while. This one did not give out a sound, seeming almost muffled even to their footsteps. They were on the last stairs. Now they stood in the gallery.

There were no boots outside the bedroom doors, such as Bill remembered seeing when he and Abraham had peeped out on to the gallery, but had gone no further. They listened most attentively, and for two or three minutes, so determined were they to be cautious. But no loud stertorous breath of any heavy sleeper reached their ears, strained to catch the faintest intrusion on the profound silence.

At last, Bill pointed to a door, as much as to say, " that's the one," and crept slowly towards it, as slowly and cautiously followed by his companion. The door was not locked, and yielded noiselessly to his hand. They both stood within the room.

" Why, there's nothing in it !" exclaimed Sam, surprised and disgusted, in a loud whisper.

"Tsh!" said Bill, with his finger on his lips, and speaking as softly and standing as near to the other as he could. "This is the room, all the same. I'll swear it is. And see there! That's the door me and Abe came through into it from the chap's bedroom."

"Well, devil a thing of any sort is there in it now but the bare walls, and we can't carry *them* off."

Bill was quite right, nevertheless, in declaring it to be the same room; and no one will be surprised that Chichester Fleetwood, impoverished as he was, should have sold everything of value that had once adorned it.

They were so disgusted, and their calculations were so utterly upset by the discovery, that they both instinctively, and at the same time, turned round towards the door by which they had entered—the door giving on to the gallery. Seeing absolutely nothing in the room itself, they were governed by a sort of reaction that made them look in precisely the opposite direction; though by doing so they merely faced the gallery out of which they had come, and which for its part offered them nothing but the spectacle of half a dozen blank and closed doors.

But just as they had done so, they both seemed to hear a sound behind them in the empty room which they had entered, and which they were about to quit. Turning again, their eyes fell upon a figure all in white, in the doorway—now open—which Bill had just identified and pointed out as "the door through which me and Abe came through from the chap's bedroom."

Far more quickly of course than this last sentence can be read, they had seen her. She had screamed and let fall the candle, and they had turned once more to the gallery and run for their lives. So eager were they to get away that they had knocked each other over in the attempt to get simultaneously through the dining-room window, which of course they had left open as a speedy means of retreat, should this become necessary, as it had now done.

They ran and ran, across the park, and over the park wall, and across fallow fields, and over a big ditch, and then through a small stream, and over a fallow field again —a good mile and a half in all—before they pulled up.   Then they stopped because they could run no further.   They were together, and no third figure was visible. They sat down side by side, and panted for breath, rubbing the sweat from their brows with their rough sleeves.

"Did you know her?" asked Bill, blowing and trembling still from exertion and terror combined.   "Did you know her again?"

"Know her again?   Do you think it was her?"

"It was her, or her wraith, one or t'other."

"I thought it was her wraith, sure enough, at first; and that made me cut harder nor anything else."

12—2

"Ay, and so did I. But wraiths don't carry candlesticks—anyways, I never heard o' none on 'em doing such—and they don't scream neither ; leastways, not in the human sort o' way she screamed."

" Wasn't it just such a scream as she screamed the night we lifted her up i' the wood at Dipleydale?"

" Just such another for all the world. I knowed her by it at once."

" Ay, but I knowed her face too, for all she were only in her bed-gown, as far as I could make out."

" I'd swear to her out of a thousand."

" So would I, lad, in any court o' justice at any 'sizes in the country."

" I've come away without my boots, I declare !"

" So have I, for the matter o' that. Wonder is they didn't follow us."

" Happen they did. We must ha' woke the whole house among us. What wi' her scream and the din we must ha' made in cutting away, they must all ha' been stirred."

"Ay, but we ran so hard, how could they catch us? We're safe enough now, I fancy. But I was rare and afeard."

These were the first considerations that presented themselves to the minds of Bully Bill and Sam Slaughterous. But the next day, when sunlight had laid all their fears of wraiths and nocturnal apparitions, another much more important consideration thrust itself on their minds.

If this was the girl they had been hired to carry off by force at Dipleydale—and neither of them had the slightest doubt upon the subject—they were probably on the traces of the man who had, through Abraham, engaged them to do so. The house where they now found her was Fleetwood Manse. The owner of that house, they well knew, was Chichester Fleetwood. It was Chichester Fleetwood then who had abducted the girl. This seemed perfectly plain.

They had not very shrewd heads for putting two and two together; but they tried to think the matter out coolly and to

help each other to fathom it still further,
and by degrees they arrived at one or two
more conclusions, which seemed to them, if
not quite so certain, at least highly probable.

But they found that more thinking and
more fathoming only muddled them. One
fact alone stood out clearly, at the end of
their thinking as at the beginning, and this
was that it must have been Mr. Fleetwood
for whom they had been employed to carry
off the girl. And this was about the only
thing, it seemed to them, worth knowing.

"Why," asked Bill, in a triumphant
manner, "if the gent was so anxious as we
should not know who he was, shouldn't it
be a fine thing for us to have found it out,
and to know it? If he weren't afraid o'
being known to us, why did he hide hisself?
And if he were afraid then, he'll be afraid
still, and we can squeeze him hard, or it's a
pity. And if Mr. Fleetwood was the gent,
why, here we've got him—for he's like to be
here—and we can squeeze him just as hard
as ever we like."

It never occurred to Bully Bill or to his comrade, that if it was Chichester Fleetwood who had thus employed them, through Abraham, he might perhaps know that they were the same fellows who had committed the first burglary in his house, and that therefore, instead of their squeezing him as they proposed, he might recognise them and hand them over again to the confinement from which they had escaped. For it must be borne in mind that though Fleetwood sat through the whole trial on the bench, next to the judge's side, and was the real prosecutor in the case, he was not called into the witness-box, not being in any way required for the purposes of proof. And as, upon that occasion, the attention of the prisoners had been completely absorbed by the various personages—the judge, the prosecuting counsel, Lord Rendover, Fleetwood's servant, the detective, &c.,—who had taken an active part in the proceedings against them, they were perfectly ignorant of Chichester

Fleetwood's appearance. Not knowing him by sight, they fell into the easy supposition that he would equally not know them.

But if they were, as they phrased it, to squeeze him, they must perforce get at him somehow; and in order to get at him, they must become acquainted with his personal appearance. This, however, they could easily gather in the neighbourhood. As soon as they succeeded in doing this, they could hang about the place for him; and if any gentleman answering to the description could be met with by them in or near to the park, they might fairly conclude that it was Chichester Fleetwood. Then they could waylay him with their threats, and extract from his fears a purchase for their silence far more valuable than anything they could have hoped to gain by the burglary, had it in itself turned out successful instead of breaking down.

Thus looked at, matters seemed to them exceedingly promising. There was not much fear of their being suspected of the last attempt. They had seen the girl, but she had not seen them, for they had had their masks on. When their first alarms had cooled down, they congratulated themselves on their failure, and came to the conclusion that the discovery which they had made would turn out the "best thing" they had ever had yet.

They little imagined that they were not only completely out in their calculations, but that they were being closely watched by their old pal and betrayer, "that brute Abe."

CHAPTER IX.

ON THE WRONG SCENT.

WHEN Lord Rendover had left Miss Blessington's presence, after the terrible rebuff which had been the reply to his pretensions for her hand, he was full, as it will be remembered, of the conviction that she was attached to Chichester Fleetwood, and that she had treated him with such severity and scorn, because he had been instrumental in bringing about Fleetwood's ruin. She had made no allusion whatsoever, in her contemptuous words, to his cousin Percy. She had dwelt solely upon the wrong done to him whom she had spoken of enthusiastically as "that noble gentleman."

Despite, therefore, Chichester Fleetwood's

financial breakdown, Lord Rendover felt as though he had reason to fear him still; and the humiliation which he had just suffered at her hands, made him add hate to fear of the man whom it seemed to him she had preferred to himself.

His exclamation uttered upon reaching the street, and repeated to himself more than once in the cab on his way home— "He shall marry Jessie! He shall marry her at once, or I'll post him as a defaulter on Monday morning," was no mere momentary resolve of idle passion. It expressed his set determination to avail himself of what seemed a splendid opportunity for gratifying his revenge and strengthening his own security at the same time.

And had Chichester Fleetwood accepted the bitter terms? He had. It seemed to him that he had no option. In any case, he was ruined. But honourable men had been ruined before. True. But had they ever been posted at Tattersall's, on every betting course, and indeed through the length and

breadth of the land, as defaulters? Had
society—and think what a terrible thing
society was in the eyes of Chichester Fleetwood!—had society ever known this of one
of its members, and not cast him forth and
branded him as a scoundrel?

He pleaded for time. He would go and
make money and pay Rendover as soon as
ever he could. No; the money at once, or
the acceptance of the bitter terms, also at
once, or—on Monday morning his name to
be classed with the blacklegs of the land!

There was no time for hesitation or effort
or ingenuity. He must marry some one
whom he had never seen, and whom he could
not but suppose was unworthy and unfit to
be any man's wife, and with her receive a
full quittance of the debt and so avoid
public disgrace; or he must refuse, and be
branded before the world as a reckless
gamester and scoundrel.

He must choose between public infamy
or private dishonour. He was a vain man.
He was a man at the mercy of public

opinion. He lived in the light and atmosphere of what others thought. Others might not think very highly of such a marriage. Yes, but he could hide that from their knowledge, and Rendover went so far as to promise that he would not divulge it. But, if he refused, others would know that he owed Rendover thirty or forty thousand pounds for a bet and could not pay him. And what would " others " think of that?

He agreed to accept the hard conditions, and the whole debt was cancelled. The marriage took place at once, of course with complete privacy and secrecy, and with the aid of a special licence. Within a very few days after, Rendover learned that Miss Blessington was engaged to Percy, that Godiva had been right, that his own suspicions had been completely erroneous, and that all he had gained by the forced marriage was to get rid of a girl whom he regarded as both a danger and a nuisance. This, however, was something.

But if Lord Rendover had heard of

Gertrude's engagement to Percy, Chichester Fleetwood had not. He had left London before it was known, and had never been in or near it since. Whither had he gone? Everybody was asking the question, and nobody was able to answer it. At last people gave up inquiring or even caring, as is the habit in the world when folks go away and stay away. Only when some stray individual still asked, "Where on earth is Chichester Fleetwood?" they got the same answer as it will be remembered Percy received at his club and repeated to his wife.

"Oh, they say he's living down at Fleetwood Manse all alone. He's ruined, you know; so what the deuce can he do?"

He was living down at Fleetwood Manse, and had been ever since his disappearance from public view. It was also true that he was living all alone, though not quite in the sense in which they who said so intended it.

Up to the precise moment of the private but strictly legal form which made Jessie

Shoreham his wife, he had never set eyes upon her; and from that moment to the present day, he had never set eyes upon her again. She had been taken down to Fleetwood Manse at once, and he had followed in her track. They were both under the same roof, but they never met. Her wants were seen to, just as his were, but that was all.

The one hasty glance that he had taken at her, whilst they were being bound by law to each other for life, was enough to satisfy him of her beauty. But this only made matters worse. He had seen the face of her who was now his wife, had recognised that it was strikingly well-favoured, and had it ever after before his eyes as plainly as though he had seen it a thousand times. Its physical charms were graven distinctly on his memory; but with those charms he therefore all the more absolutely and certainly connected what he naturally concluded was her disgrace and his dishonour.

He hated her. She was the instrument of his humiliation. She could not have

been forced, he argued, as he had been
forced, to accept the bitter conditions. She,
perforce, had been free, and had willingly
entered into the plot with Rendover, in
order that both might profit by his degrada-
tion. She had married him, of course, for
ambition. Ruined as he was for the moment, he was still a magnificent match for a
creature such as she must be.

She had thought to play her own game
admirably at the same time that she con-
sented to play Rendover's. But, if Rendover
had not been foiled, she should be. His
wife she might be, legally, and he would
give her the shelter and maintenance to
which she had a right. Having that, she
might go her own way. He would never
treat her as his wife. She should never
communicate with him more.

All his old staff of servants were dismissed. Economy required that much.
Horses were sold, carriages were sold, and
the place was given up to the slow but
insidious tooth of undisturbed time and

silence. He shut himself completely up, choosing for his own room the big library. It was bedroom and sitting-room to him both. He never stirred from it.

There immured, he moodily meditated over his wrongs and his misfortunes. It seemed to him as if Heaven and earth had combined and conspired against him. He regarded himself as watched, laid in wait for, and caught, pursued and flogged, by Fate. No blunders of his own had brought about his doom. No common mischance could have done it. He was the sport of malicious fortune, the victim of a superhuman malice and skill.

He had spent the earlier years of his manhood in distant travel, courageous adventure, unflagging energy, and multifarious enterprise, and at last found himself, in its zenith, wealthy, honoured, and influential. Suddenly he had been toppled down; down to a depth far below that from which he had commenced his younger struggles; a depth from which there was no rising.

Even were it possible to rise again, was it any longer worth while to try? If he succeeded, success would still find him clogged with—his wife. How could he comfort himself during the struggle? Worse still: how could he comfort himself when the struggle was over and was successful? To succeed now would only be to blazon before all the world his irretrievable disgrace. And that world would then know not only whom he had married, but why he had married her. They knew neither now. No. Struggle was useless. Complete seclusion, death in life, absolute renunciation of everything, was the only course left open to him. As long as Lord Rendover and his own wife lived, there was no outlook for him.

He saw nobody, he corresponded with nobody, he inquired of nobody. He read no newspapers. He received none. He was in the very midst of hundreds of books, and he never opened one of them. He was surrounded by a good-sized park, and he never put foot beyond the house.

The autumn months passed away, and the winter had come, and he looked ten or fifteen years older. His erect carriage had left him. He stooped like a life-long student, and his handsome brown beard was streaked with grey. All kindness had gone out of his face. His look was a stare, his soliloquy was a mumble.

By degrees his vague inner accusations against Fate had grown more fixed and definite, and his hatred fastened itself more concentratedly on Lord Rendover and her whom he tried to think of not as his wife, but as "that girl." If he could be avenged upon them. If he could rid the world, and therefore himself, of either or both.

By the time that the new year—unknown to him, for he had kept no count—had come for the rest of mankind, he could scarcely be said to retain full possession of his faculties. Never an intellectual man at all, and always dependent for the exercise of his brain, even to the small extent to which he had ever exercised it, upon the provocation and encouragement of others, he was in his seclusion rapidly slipping into a state that, if yet quite different from what is ordinarily meant by idiocy, had already in appearance something in common with it, and might end by having everything in common with it in reality. He wanted to be avenged and to be free, and he was in the poorest possible state of mind for working out either end. Even his desire for personal revenge could not be said to be very intense, whilst his means for attaining it were miserably small.

Arrived at this frame of general impotence and despondency, it was not wonderful that he should accept any apparent instrument of vengeance that thrust itself upon him. Able to find none of himself, he was at the mercy of any accidental temptation that might fall in his way. After long but nothing like concentrated reflection, the only result of which was that he arrived at the perception of his own powerlessness, a small incident that happened some time at the commencement of February, threw in his path what seemed to him might possibly furnish him with the means of punishing one if not both of his main enemies, and emancipating himself from the thraldom of each.

It was very simple, and it was this. He used to spend much time in pacing up and down the large room which he inhabited, and more particularly of a night when day-light was gone and its place was supplied by only two candles that stood on a table almost in the centre of the library. He had grown more and more absent, and more and more careless in his steps, and would infallibly have constantly been knocking up against chairs or pieces of furniture had there been more of these to knock against.

On the night referred to, however, in the course of his perambulations, he nearly fell over something, and hurt himself severely. But for the pain he would merely have gone on and taken no notice. Smarting, however, as he was, he turned to see what had occa-sioned the obstruction, and even went so far

as to move it a little out of the way, and put
it further back into a recess near to which it
already stood. It was only a medicine chest,
placed there doubtless since he had chosen
to turn the library into his sitting-room and
bedroom alike.

But when he had placed it in the recess,
he seemed to change his mind. He lifted it
up again, carried it towards the table on
which the candles were burning, placed it
hard by the table and the chair which he
invariably occupied, sat down, drew one of
the candles nearer to it and to himself,
opened it, and began examining its contents
carefully.

At last he paused, for he had found what he
wanted. It was a drug that had been given
him in the East, with even whose name or
properties he was unacquainted, but which
he had been assured was a rare and subtle
poison. If he could only find out its pecu-
liarities, might he not yet be avenged?
This was his sorry idea. For the moment
it went no further.

How was he to discover its properties and its action? This was the next thought that presented itself to him. Not far from his feet was lying, fast asleep, an old pointer which had been shot in the stubble field a couple of years ago, and was now stone blind. Ever since his return to the Manse, and his resolute seclusion, poor old Truro had stuck closely to him. It had immediately divined his return, had followed him to the library, and had shared his confinement ever since. It had stayed with him, and pined with him, as though they had both been smitten by one and the same blow.

Time was when he would have been struck and gratified by such a preference and such fidelity. But now he accepted the dog's constant presence because he found it there. If ever anything passed between the two prisoners, it was because the dog noticed him, not because he noticed the dog.

Why should he not try the effects of the poison upon the blind old pointer? The notion of returning power, of having some object to effect and also the power to effect it, seized hold of him, and he soon began his experiments. They were clumsy and even ridiculous. They went on, day after day, though somewhat irregularly, for more than a fortnight, producing no visible result in the eyes of the poor unskilled operator, save an appearance of pleasure on the part of old Truro, as being more noticed and, as it seemed to the dog, played with.

So altered, and weakened, and indeed shattered was his mind, that he soon quite forgot the motive which had first driven him to experiment upon the animal. His mind could no longer harbour two thoughts at a time, or a complex thought at all. He had positively forgotten all about his own fate, and his enemies, and his desire to be avenged upon them, in the one interest that by this time had exclusively settled upon him, to see what result his drug would have upon the blind pointer. He did notice that the drug was getting gradually consumed; but it did not any longer in the least occur to him that, if it came to be consumed entirely, the experiment would have been utterly thrown away.

So thoroughly dead was he to this, and so completely had he, even in the space of two or three weeks, outgrown his original motive, that at last he one night gave the dog all that remained; about four times as much as he had ever given it before at a single time.

The pointer very soon waxed exuberantly playful, and jumped and skipped about and manifested in every way its joy at being more than usually noticed by its companion and master. It at length forced him into romping with it—not as he once would have done, but to the best of his ability, and far more vivaciously than he had ever done since their joint confinement had commenced.

At length Truro stopped in his play, and so did his master; falling back, almost exhausted with the unusual exertion, into his chair. It then came to his feet, seemed to try to get its paws on to his knees, failed to do so, yawned widely, whined, lay on its back, had convulsions that lasted about eight seconds, and then rolled over and lay perfectly still. The blind old pointer was dead.

He called it, but it no longer answered to his voice. He stooped down and patted it. Still no response. He shook it; but it lay, when he withdrew his hand, just where his hand had left it. The real truth crept slowly over his mind; the faithful creature was dead. He called aloud its name over and over again, in a tone of pain and fearful hope, as though so calling would revive it. Then it struck him that he—he himself—had killed it.

A flood of emotion, alien to everything he had felt for months, rushed through him. How had he killed it? Why had he killed it? This last question, this terrible "why," brought suddenly back to his consciousness what he had entirely put out of sight. He had poisoned it, in seeking to find out how he could be avenged upon his enemies. How? He could not face the thought. The mere remembrance, in this moment of new emotion, of his having ever housed such a scheme in his brain, filled him with horror, and redoubled the tender feelings which were already possessing him. He buried his face in his hands. He was physically as well as mentally weakened. He burst into tears, and sobbed like a child.

When this fit passed away, there came upon him a burning desire to stand in the sunlight, in the full light of day, with the pure free air around him. He rushed to the window, and tore open the shutters. It was night. He opened the window. It was almost pitch dark; but at least the fresh, unblemished air came against his face, and he felt relieved and, as it were, revived. Would that the day would break! He would do what he had not done for months. He would court the healing of the open sunshine.

There lay the dog upon the ground, dead.
The sight kept alive the shock that he had at
first received.   He was horrified at the stage
at which he had arrived, and to which long
brooding in solitude and confinement had
brought him.   He stood, and tried to think
clearly.   Was he mad?   Was there any
fear that he had gone mad?

No. He was sane, perfectly sane. He
felt sure of that.   The dog lay dead, and
the past was very terrible; but, thank God!
he was yet quite in his senses. He might
have gone mad had this lasted much longer.
As it was, however, he was saved.   But he
must no more expose himself to the risk
incident to such conditions as those which
he had of late been imposing upon himself.
No more close confinement.   No more
brooding.

He fell asleep in his chair whilst waiting
for the morning. When he awoke it was
far advanced.   It was a lovely day, belonging half to lingering winter, half to
approaching spring.

About half-past eleven, his servant was surprised to meet him in the hall, the front door of which stood open; so balmy and mild was the morning.

"What day of the month is it?" he asked.

"The twenty-fifth, sir," answered the servant.

"The twenty-fifth of——?" And he paused.

The servant understood, and replied, quietly—

"The twenty-fifth of February, sir."

"Yes, yes, the twenty-fifth of February. Of course it is."

He passed out through the hall-door into the park, where the sun was shining gloriously, the birds were ecstatically singing, the tender buds were beginning to take heart and shoot, and the air smelt of the sweet moist scent of returning life.

"The twenty-fifth of February," he repeated to himself. "From August to February, one, two, three—six months.

Yes, six. It 'can't be another year. No, there hasn't been a summer between. Six months; February—February the twenty-fifth. How beautiful!"

He halted, and looked around. His face was bathed in a glow of sentimental tenderness. The tears swam in his eyes. Again he said—-

"How beautiful!" And then he walked on again.

He walked very slowly; but, at last, he reached a spot which had always been a favourite one with him. It was on the main pathway that led round the park, but inside of it;·a narrow but thick plantation lying between it and the park fence. There had always been a wooden seat there, for from it was obtained the most extensive view of the park, and also the best one of the Manse. The seat was there still, though it was rotting from neglect.

He sat down. Before him was what was left of his own and his ancestors' possessions. He was not thinking of these, however.

He was surrendering himself wholly to
the sunshine, and to the blithe singing
that was going on above and behind him ;
more blithe even than elsewhere, since there
the plantation was thickest, being formed
mostly of holly and evergreens, and the
sparkling brushwood that never sheds its
leaves. He sat down, and he felt at peace.

He had not been there long before a
couple of men clomb the park fence from
without, one of them about twenty yards to
the right, the other about an equal distance
to the left of where he sat, but both, of
course, behind him. Had he been the most
attentive watcher for sounds, instead of
being absorbed in the bright landscape and
the sweet carolling and his own deep, calm,
passive, tender joy, it is probable that he
would not have heard their first movements.
But even they themselves were surprised
when, after creeping under the surmounted
park paling to meet each other midway, and
together approaching through the plantation to within twelve or fourteen feet of his

back, they still seemed not to disturb him.
His remaining so quiet had the effect of
making them pause, and also stand perfectly
still for a minute or so.

They had contrived to pick up a description of him, and it tallied completely with
just so much as they had seen of the unknown gentleman at Dipleydale. The
reader doubtless remembers how when Lord
Rendover—in reality closely shorn, save on
the upper lip—turned away from Jessie
towards the little bridge and whistled,
though in a purposely feigned direction, as
a sign to the men to rush out and seize her,
he hastily put on a large beard and
whiskers; so that when he turned, and in
the deeper than twilight gave them his brief
orders to follow him, he presented to
them the appearance of a man with
abundance of hair on his cheeks and chin.
Such was Chichester Fleetwood described to
them as having, and such was the man now
on the seat before them. Moreover, he was
spoken of as tall. Tall too was the man in

the Dipleydale woods ; and tall too, though sitting down, was the man to whom they now approached nearer, and whom, in a few seconds more, they both stood confronting.

"Maybe you don't know us, Mr. Fleetwood?" said Stebbins.

He had seen them, it is true, a year ago, in the dock at the assizes, and had, of course, taken good note of them, though, as has been explained, they took no note of him there whatsoever. But they were both considerably altered since then, both by the prison discipline they had gone through, and by devices of course not neglected by themselves. Besides, on that occasion—the only one on which he had ever before seen them—they were uncovered. Now they had their wide-awakes on. If to all this be added what he himself had gone through, and the present poor state of his memory, both in its retentive and its reproductive capacity, it is not wonderful that he should have stared at them vaguely, and answered calmly—

"No, indeed, I do not.   Neither of you."

By his answer, however, he had responded to the name by which they had addressed him, that of Mr. Fleetwood.   He was then the man whom they were seeking.

"But *we* know *you*, Mr. Fleetwood," said Speke.

"That we do," added Stebbins, doggedly, "and I think you'll soon find you know more about us than you pretend to, or than perhaps 'll prove convenient to you.   Maybe you don't know one Abraham Coggett neither."

"I can't say I do," he answered, placidly. "Stay"—and he raised his hand to his brow, as men do when they search their memory intently.   "Coggett—Coggett.   I seem to know the name.   I've heard the name somewhere, I'm sure.   Let me see.   Coggett —Coggett.   No, it's no use.   It's gone; it's gone.   But I've heard it somewhere."

He had heard it, of course, at the trial, when Abraham had been called into the witness-box and examined.

"Then I think we'd better jog your

memory, Mr. Fleetwood. Mayhap, you've heard of such a place as Dipleydale?"

" Yes, it's a pretty place down in the west of England, is it not?"

" Well, rather. And I suppose you never was there, yoursen?"

" No, I never was, though I have heard of it, I say."

" He's a cool 'un, Bill, isn't he?"

He still remained seated, leaning forward rather and resting part of the weight of his body on his stick, upon the handle of which his hands were crossed. He seemed neither irritated nor alarmed by their rude questioning. His manner was certainly calculated to disconcert them, and to shake the conviction of men more intelligent or less dogged. But they were not so easily to be balked.

" Well, Mr. Fleetwood," one of them continued, " we think you *have* been at Dipleydale, you see; and what's more, that we've been there with you, and Abram Coggett was there too."

"Ay, and somebody else was there, and that somebody was a girl as you was a-coorting, and as you couldn't get her to go off wi' you, you got that same Abram to get us to carry her off for you. Now, you see, we know all about it, Mr. Fleetwood, and it's no use your pretending not to know anything about it, for we've got the proofs of it all, and by ——, if you don't come out handsome, we'll use 'em, and where'll you be then?"

A fear began to creep over him, though not from anything they were saying to him. He knew well enough that what they said was not true, was, indeed, wholly without foundation. How then could they say it, and say it so positively? Was he dreaming it all, and was he the sport of some horrible creation of his own mind. The horrible thought of the preceding night came over him. Was he mad? Had he really, after all, lost his senses? But no; how could it be? He felt quite sane. Round him were the air and the sunshine; here was the broad undulating park; there stood the Manse. The landscape was stretched out before him. He knew where he was sitting, and how he had come there. He saw the two men distinctly, and heard their words quite plainly. He could not be mad. It must be they, and not he, who were the victims of some delusion.

"You are quite wrong," he said, calmly, "whatever you may think to the contrary. I never was at Dipleydale. I never carried off any girl from there or elsewhere, and I never employed anybody to do so for me. I do not know in the least who you are. I have heard the name of Abraham Coggett somewhere, but where or under what circumstances I cannot remember. Now you know all that I know; and I think you must see that you are mistaken."

"Are we, though?" said Stebbins, just as doggedly as ever.

But at that moment, they both perceived that three labourers were coming along the park pathway, probably on their way to

their midday meal, and would soon be pass-
ing the spot where they stood. They looked
at each other significantly, conveying silently
to each other the intimation that it would
be safer for them to be moving off.

" We know we're not mistaken, Mr. Fleetwood. Nothing of the kind. And we'll
show you if we are, if you wont listen to
reason, and come down handsome. We
shall look for you here again, about the
same hour; and if we don't see you very
soon, and you don't come to terms, we'll see
what the law says to gents as carries off
poor girls agin their wills, in woods, of a
dark night."

With that they passed behind him into
the plantation. He saw the labourers approaching, and guessed the cause of their
disappearance. But he too felt shy of seeing
anybody, especially labourers about his own
place, who would probably recognise him.
So he rose from his seat, and in order to
avoid being met or overtaken by them,
walked straight on towards the house across

the grass. He soon forgot the two men who had addressed him, his thoughts, or rather his feelings, once more reverting to the soft, sweet air, to the blue sky, to the many-throated music. Ever and anon he stopped, always repeating the self-same exclamation.

"How beautiful! how beautiful!"

Meanwhile, the two men who had just left him pushed their way through the plantation, and again climbed the park paling, and stood on the common outside it. Looking back over it, they saw that the labourers whose approach had disturbed them in their task of making Mr. Fleetwood "reasonable," had reached the seat where they had lately been standing by him, and had passed on without taking any notice, or indeed without looking right or left. There had been nothing to arouse their suspicions, and they were no doubt hurrying home to their cottages, their minds intent upon their coming dinner and rest. They saw also that Mr. Fleetwood had risen and was walking

across the grass of the park in the direction
of the house. But he was doing so very
leisurely. He stopped often, but never
looked back, and he was, therefore, evidently not bent on any scheme injurious to
them.

So encouraged, they drew themselves up
from their half-crouching position, and un-
concernedly rested their arms on the tops of
the paling, looking over it through the plantation into the park. Speke even went so
far as to pull out his pipe and light it.
Neither of them was consciously alive to
that ineffable something which caused Fleetwood ever and anon to exclaim, " How beautiful!" but both of them no doubt enjoyed
the quiet and the sunshine, as a dog, or a
cat, or many another animal would have enjoyed that February noon.

"It's not the chap, I fear," said Speke,
who was becoming philosophically clear-
seeing under the sobering effects of his pipe.
" It's not the chap, Bill, after all."

" It must be the chap, I say," retorted

Bill. "It's the girl, I'll swear, or eyes isn't worth having, no nor screams neither."

"Ay, lad, it's the girl sure enough," said his companion, whom all the tobacco in the world could not have cooled down into scepticism upon that point. "I'll be shot, if it isn't the girl. But it isn't the gent, all the same."

"Then who the hangman is it, Sam?" asked Bill, who seemed to think that if Speke could not answer that question satisfactorily, the "gent's" identity was fully proved.

But the pipe made his companion far too profound a logician for him to be tripped up by such an argument.

"That's more nor I know, nor you neither. But yon's not him, you may lay a crown on it. Folks can't act like that."

"Can't they, though?" said Bill. "Nobody knows where their skill in acting ends. If we're to believe that he's not the chap, because he says he ain't, we might just as well never ha' tried it on at all. You didn't think he'd own to it at wonst?"

There was something in that; and Sam, who continued quiet smoking made every moment more impartial, saw that there was. Accordingly, he did not allow himself to answer hurriedly, though Bill kept looking at him for a reply to what he conceived was a "poser." But over and above this, Sam's pipe, besides making him more reflective, had also made him more observant. So that when he did speak, it was not to answer Bill's "poser," but to say quietly—

"What's that i' the bushes, Bill?"

"I' the bushes? Where? What? I see nought."

"Why, there!" he answered, pointing with his finger. "No—to the left a little. It's moving now. If you don't see it, don't you hear it?"

All at once he had thrown off his quiet philosophic manner, and was over the fence again and inside the plantation.

From the habit of one doing whatever the other did, Bill, though still seeing nothing, was quickly over the fence after him. He saw Speke pushing straight through the brushwood, and followed straight at his comrade's heels. In a few seconds more, he saw a man crouch and Speke make a dash at him with his hand. The man ducked again and fell, leaving in Speke's hand a cap and wig. They both burst out laughing. But in another moment their faces wore an expression more earnest than that of mere merriment.

"Well, I'm blest if it ain't Abraham!" exclaimed Sam.

The loss of the red wig, the old look of mingled cunning and fear in the face of the crouching figure, combined with the situation and the attempt at concealment, all went to betray him beyond doubt or hope. His own craven nature put the finishing touch to his discovery.

"I'll tell you all. I'll tell you all, if you'll only spare me. It was Lord Rendover, it was all Lord Rendover. Don't let Bill hurt me, Sam! Save me, like a good

fellow, and I'll tell you all. It's worth no
end o' money to you; for it was all Lord
Rendover, all Lord Rendover, every bit,
and I couldn't help myself, for I was in his
power; in his power, and I could not help it."

"You're in ours now at any rate. So
come along wi' you. Here's a fine thing!"
said Sam, holding up the red wig and
showing it to Bill Stebbins. Then he
threw it and the cap contemptuously to
Abraham. "There, put it on, and let's see
how you look in it. Don't hurt him, Bill!
He'll be worth money to us, as he says.
If he isn't, time enough to give him a taste
o' your quality then."

Bill kept muttering ominously and looking at Abraham in a way that showed he
was half-inclined to sacrifice all chance of
future profit to the gratification of present
animosity. But, kept back by his more
prudent companion, he desisted from his
design of swift and personal vengeance.
Abraham meanwhile was readjusting the
red wig.

"Well, I'm blest if I ever should ha' known him in that. It's a beautiful disguise, if ever there was one. If you'd only stood straight up and not gone ducking and ducking like a bantam fowl, you'd never have lost it; and then we'd never ha' caught our bird, eh, Bill?"

But the bird was fast caught now. Hope of escape or evasion was there none. Mr. Richard Thornton fervently wished himself back in Park Lane, but all the wishing in the world would not save him now. He was irrecoverably in the hands of Bully Bill and Sam Slaughterous.

CHAPTER X.

SAVED BY FAITH.

AND was Jessie really at the Manse? Or were the two escaped felons as much mistaken about her as they evidently were in their suspicion that Chichester Fleetwood was concerned in the affair at Dipleydale?

No. They were quite right in believing that they had seen her, and seen her in the flesh on the night of the twenty-third. Having been wide awake at the time of their entry, though having some time ago retired to rest, and occupying as she did, strangely enough, the room which had been Lord Rendover's on the occasion of his visit to the Manse with which our story opened, she heard some one in the room between

hers and the main landing, and went to see
who it could be. Both the lateness of the
hour and her knowledge that the room
stood always empty, had aroused her curiosity.

The discovery which she immediately
made, followed by her scream of terror and
by her letting her candle fall, produced no
result beyond that of putting the two men to
sudden flight. There were very few persons
in the big house, and neither her screams
nor the burglars' rush to escape reached the
ears of any of them. For herself, she
hurried back to her own room as quickly
as ever she could, and locked herself in, far
too much terrified to trust herself again
beyond it.

She heard no further sound, however,
that night, but she never closed her eyes
till daylight. The sight of the two men,
even though they had turned and fled, had
filled her with horrible fears. They re-
minded her of the night in the wood, of
which she never could think without shud-

dering, when two men had laid forcible
hands on her, smothered her screams, lifted
her into the air, and borne her in violence
away.   Again two men were seeking her
out.   Again, therefore, violence must be
meditated against her.

Why then, on seeing her, had they fled?
A still more horrible thought flashed across
her brain.   They had come to murder her,
but to murder her in darkness and in silence.
They had imagined she would be fast
asleep at that hour, and their purpose had
been to enter and murder her in her slumber,
or in the instant of her waking.   They had
fled, because they feared her screams would
be heard by some of the servants.   They
had therefore postponed their bloody intent.

But if they wanted to murder her, what
was their motive?   They were employed to
do so, just as the other two men had been
employed to abduct her at Dipleydale.   By
whom could they be employed?   By the
same man, perhaps in league with Mr. Fleetwood to whom that man had married her,

and whom she had never seen since.
Clearly they had schemes in common.   Probably they had this last one in common;
and it was to make away with her.

These were her thoughts all night
through, in that big dreary, lonely house,
a large part of which she had never seen,
and where she was living practically all
alone.   There was the big, silent house, and
outside the big silent park, and outside that
again, the big terrible world, in which she
had not a friend nor an acquaintance, and
people in it were conspiring to murder
her.

Morning, however, brought some mitiga-
tion of her fears. Firstly, there was the day-
light, the bright, happy, unmurderous day-
light, and before it terrors born of nocturnal
hours and depths of silence, perforce flee
away in part.   But shortly it also brought
the maid-servant and her busy tattle.   There
had been burglars during the night, she
said.   The dining-room window had been
left open; and so eager had the men been

to get away that they had left their boots behind them. Beyond this, however, the girl had nothing to tell.

This much, however, was exceedingly reassuring to Jessie. She breathed not a syllable of the fears which had racked her during the night, and her own good sense helped to banish them more or less from her own bosom. Still when night again came round, she naturally enough had a recurrence of her fears; not so intensely as before, but still in a form hard enough to bear and to suppress. She took more than usual care to see that the door leading into the empty room was locked. But it will be remembered from the description given both at the time of Lord Rendover's occupying the room and at the trial, that it had another door, immediately opposite the one to whose security she was seeing; a door which led first into a little ante-room, and then through double folding-doors into the library. To the door which led into the little ante-room there was no lock, but the first folding-doors were fastened, though not from her side, and had been so fastened ever since her arrival. She did not even know what there was on the other side of it; but she felt no alarm or fear of her room being invaded from that quarter. Her whole nervousness lay in the other direction from which well-grounded alarm had once come, and that as recently as the previous night.

However, she was not disturbed on the succeeding one. Not the less, however, on the following night again—that is on the twenty-fifth—did she omit any precaution. She locked, and unlocked, and relocked, and tried and tried again, the door which led into the empty and despoiled room. This she did as early as nine o'clock, though she had as yet no intention of retiring to rest. But, about half-an-hour afterwards, she thought she heard a door being tried. She rushed to the one she had so carefully fastened. She was in an agony of terror. All her first suspicions returned. Here

15—2

again were the men; here, at last, her mur-
derers.   Should she scream?   No; she
thought she had better listen first.   It was
not the door close to which she was standing that was being forced; nor yet could
she feel sure that anybody was on the other
side of it at all.   Still she heard sounds;
and now sounds of a door yielding.   She
would rush to her window, open it, and
shout at the top of her voice.   She turned
to do so, when to her horror she saw at the
same moment the door right opposite to
her—the door without a lock—being opened.
She was lost now.   She felt that her last
hour had come, and she stood bound to the
spot.   The door opened fully; and before
her stood—Mr. Fleetwood!

The February sunshine had done its holy
work.   The pure air of Heaven, the wholesome landscape, the soothing insinuating
song of vernal birds, had wrought their cure.
He had passed in from them all, at length,
and returned to the big, dreary library.
But their sacred influence quietly pursued

him, and his heart flowed with streams of tenderness all the more full and free for its long drought. He thought not of the men who had just accosted him. He thought not of Rendover. He thought not even of his wrong. His softened emotions led him to think of a girl who, for anything he knew, might be as wretched as himself, and about whose state he had never even inquired. He knew that she was under his roof, but he knew no more.

Would it not be better, juster, kinder, to see her, to hear what she had to say for herself, and then to try to make her life pleasanter to her, even though he could never consent to allow it to be spent with his? To all these questions, the sunlight, and the blue sky, and the innocent bird-twittering, gave but one silent yet overpowering reply.

He wished that the interview should be unknown to any one until he saw what ensued from it. Accordingly, he had waited till night, and had chosen his present

method of finding himself in her presence.

" I believe you are my wife ?" he said.

" Yes, sir !" she answered, " I am."

A fresh though a different fear had been
suddenly superadded to her original one.
She trembled all over, and now her face
was suffused with blushes.

" Pardon my disturbing you thus," he
went on.   "I thought it the best way of
seeing you for the present."

" Whatever you think best, is best,"
she answered.   "You cannot ask pardon of me.   I will do whatever you wish,
sir !"

These were the first words that had ever
passed between them.   He was overcome
with amazement at them, at their tone, at
her manner, at her blushes, her nervousness, her meek humility.

" Have you been here ever since you
came here first?" he asked.

" Yes, sir !   Since you sent me here last
August."

"But you have been out of the house, have you not?"

"Yes, sir, often. When I first came—in the autumn, sir—I almost lived in the park. Often during the winter I could not go out; but I have done so every day whenever I could. Have I done wrong?"

And she glanced timidly towards him.

"Certainly not. But have you never been further than that?"

"Yes, sir, sometimes, but not very far. I was frightened."

"But have you never gone away, I mean, for a time?"

"No, sir, never. You never said I might."

What a world of reproaches was contained in those simple words, little as they were intended to be reproachful!

"And have you had nobody to come and see you—no friends—no relations?"

The tears came into her eyes, but she contrived to stay their advance.

"Who would want to come and see me?

I have no friends, no relations. I have seen no one since I came, but three servants."

" And why have you stayed here all this time?" he asked.

" Because it was my duty, sir! At least, I thought it was. And I thought — I thought"—here she hesitated—" perhaps I thought——"

" Tell we what you thought," he said, encouraging her.

" I thought perhaps that you would come —come some day or other—and—and speak to me, and—and then—then learn the truth."

" Will you tell me the truth—the whole truth," he said, " if I ask you to tell it me now ?"

" Yes, sir, I will. But I do not think you will believe me."

" Let me hear it," he said, gravely, almost ·a little harshly, " and then I shall be better able to judge."

" But where shall I begin? I don't know where to begin. I don't know, sir,

what you know, and what you don't know.
Please ask me something."

"Do you know why I married you?" he
asked, plainly.

"No, sir, not in the least. How could I
know?"

"Did Lord Rendover never tell you why?
And if he did not, what *did* he tell you?"

"He did not tell me anything. I know
nothing about you, except your name, and
that you live here, and that you sent me
here also."

"Do you mean to tell me that? Will
you swear it?"

"If you wish it, sir, I will; for it is true,"
she answered, simply.

He looked at her, as though he wanted
to get inside her mind, and know for certain
that this was true. Yet who could refuse
to believe her, standing there meekly and
speaking thus ingenuously as she was?

"Then why did *you* marry *me?* Answer
me that," he said, severely.

"Because, sir, I thought it was the best

thing I could do, and having no reason to suppose that you had any objection to it."

"Why was it the best thing you could do? But no: I can understand easily enough why it was the best thing for you to do."

"No, sir, you do not. At least I think you do not," she replied, with a look of increasing pain and confusion. "But if I told you the real reason, you would not believe it. There's where it is," she added, in a tone of bitter despondency.

"Tell me, at any rate. I will listen to it all."

"But I must tell you my whole story."

"Do so, then."

"But how much of it do you know already? Or how much do you think you know? for what you have been told must be false."

"I know nothing, and have been told nothing. All that I know is that I married you because I was obliged, and because Lord Rendover wanted to get rid of you."

"Oh dear, oh dear!" she wailed. "I thought it was so. I had begun of late to suspect it was so. I did not suspect it at first, or I assure you, sir—I assure you, sir!—I would not have done it. Had I known what you tell me now, I would not have helped him—indeed I would not, sir! I would have gone on enduring my position. But I thought you wished it somehow, and I thought it would be the best thing for me. But you do not believe me. I see that you do not believe me. Who would?"

The old terror was upon her; the terror of feeling that she had been grievously wronged, and never could prove it.

"I cannot know, till you tell me all. Tell it me from first to last."

She did her best. It was not easy, but she tried. The beginning too was the worst part of it; for there she had to confess her own faults—not more than faults, if you like, but still faults, her own faults—her vanity, her love of pleasure, her weariness at Netwold Farm, her sighing for

some excitement, her yielding to the promise or hope of change, even though it
came without proper credentials, and was
accepted under conditions of secrecy that
she knew were blameable. But she con-
fessed all this, not trying in the least to
extenuate her weakness, her want of
staunch devotion to duty, her wicked
blinding of her Aunt Mary and her Uncle
Roger.

"But I thought he would marry me,"
she went on. "He told me he would
marry me. He swore that he would. I
did not know who he was; he did not tell
me who he was at first. It was only when
I said that I could not go away with him,
without first being married to him, that he
made any difficulties. I could not get him
to yield. But I was resolved not to yield
either."

"But you did yield at last?"

"Oh no, sir! I did not, indeed I did
not. You will not believe it, I know you
will not believe it; but for all that I did

not. He swore that he would marry me at once, and immediately after would let my Aunt Mary know. But I would not listen to him, for I knew that would be wrong. I had done enough wrong already, and I did not want to do any more. Indeed, sir, I did not yield."

" Then what happened ?" he asked.

She told him ; narrating the story as best she could, in her simple monosyllabic way. How she had gone to say good-bye to him for ever, resolved never to see him more, giving him back his notes and his presents. How, just as we already know, she had met him in the wood, as she meant, for the last time. How, in fine, she had been seized and borne off by main force.

" And you mean to say that Lord Rendover carried you off by violence ?"

" Yes, sir, indeed he did, I assure you he did; and then what could I do ? I insisted upon his taking me back home, and telling everybody what he had done. But he

would not. He would do everything on
earth for me, he said, but he could not do
that."

"But why did you not go back alone?"

"They would not have received me; or
if they had, they would not have believed
me, and I should have been disgraced with
them for ever. I had met him in the
woods, three or four times, and always—
always in secret; and I should have had to
say this, and to confess all; and then who
would have believed that I had been carried
off by force? How could I have proved it?
He would have gone away. He was rich
and powerful.   What could I do?"

"What did you do then?" he asked
with lowering brows.

"I said he must either take me back
home, or he must marry me at once. He
would marry me later, he said. It was a
thing that could not be done in a day. He
would do it as quickly as it could be
managed. He swore that he loved me,
and said that I ought to be kind to him

and help him, instead of making difficulties."

"And *did* you love him?" asked her pitiless
interrogator.

" No, sir, I did not. I was frightened of
him, but I had not the least feeling of
love for him, since he had treated me so.
I wanted to be able to love him a little, for
I was so frightened of him; but I could
not. He was very kind to me at first, or
pretended to be so. But when he found
that kindness was no good, and that I
would not listen to him until he married
me, he was not so kind. Sometimes he
was, and sometimes he wasn't."

" And where did he take you to?"

" He had taken me up to a cottage near
London, through which we passed on our
way to it. He got me to go there, because
he said that there it would be easier for us
to be married. But when we got there he
made fresh difficulties, and got more angry
with me because he could not make me
give in. He swore again he would marry

me in the end, if I would make no more
bother, he said, at present.   But at present
he could not marry me.   Then I told him
that I was quite sure that he never intended
to marry me, and that he did not intend to
do so."

"How long after his carrying you off did
you tell him that?"

"About six weeks, sir, I think.   I had
been trying to hope, and to believe him, all
that time; for not hoping or believing any
more was so terrible.   But I did not hope
or believe any longer, and I told him so.
Then he lost his temper, and said I was a
little fool if I had ever expected anything
of the kind; that he was very fond of me,
and would make me very happy, but that
he never could marry me, and the sooner I
got the idea out of my head the better."

When she had got thus far, she could
repress her tears no longer, and all that she
said afterwards was mingled with spasmodic
sobbing.

"Then, sir, I got a servant of his

who was kind to me, or who seemed to be——"

"Did you know who he really was by this time?"

"Oh, yes, sir, I knew it then. I got this servant to go to Dipleydale, and hear what the people said there about me, and what Aunt Mary thought, and Uncle Roger, and everybody. And he went, and he came back, sir, and he told me that they all said I had gone away with a gentleman with whom I had been seen talking in the wood after sundown, and nobody had heard of me since. And oh, sir! he told me that Aunt Mary—that Aunt Mary and Uncle Roger— that they both said—said—said I was no good—no good—and they never wanted —never wanted to hear of me again."

She covered her poor tear-streaked face with her hands, and shook and sobbed aloud; sobbed as she had sobbed at the cottage near Bracknell, when she had first heard the words, and had reiterated them over and over again to herself in the sum-

mer night, and there were none but the
nightingales to hear her.

"And then, sir, I gave in, and hoped no
more."

"You gave in to him!" said a deep,
solemn, accusing voice.

"Oh, no, sir!" she exclaimed, withdraw-
ing her hands from her face, and indignant
horror flashing through her streaming
tears, and even staying for a moment their
constant course. "Not to *him*. I did not
give in to *him*. Never, never! I gave up
hoping, I mean. I knew it was all over,
and there was no more hope, and that I
was doomed to be miserable for ever.
Again, and again, and again, I begged him
to help me to go home, to go with me there
to tell them the truth, to get the men who
helped him to go also, and for them also
to tell the truth, and then, perhaps, I
should be believed. Or if he would not,
let him marry me still, and I would then
go away, and he should never hear of me
again, and I never would bother him more.

But he would not. He tried to force me to go and live in London, but I would not go. I knew now that he wanted to ruin me in some way or other, and I was obstinate, and was determined to make no more blunders, if I could help it."

She stopped again, and dried her tears, thinking he, perhaps, would ask her something more, and so help her to go on with her story. But he stood looking at her, looking her through and through, not with pity in his face, not with scorn, not with doubt; simply looking at her.

" At last," she resumed, " having failed in every way, and wishing to get rid of me, I suppose, he asked me if I would marry— not him, but anybody else. Not somebody in particular, but anybody at all. I was worn out, I was without hope, and I clutched at that gleam of it. I said I would marry anybody, anybody, but I hoped he would not be wicked, and I begged that he might not be cruel. I was afraid it would be somebody who was cruel, and

I had suffered so much already, I did not want him to be that. And then—then, sir!—I know no more. I believed I married you, sir; and I beg your pardon, and if I had known you did not wish it, I would not have done it. And I hope you forgive me, and I'll do anything you like, and I'll go away, and never bother you any more, sir, if you'll only take me back to Aunt Mary and say that I am your wife, and try to make her believe that I'm an honest girl; for if she believes it, Uncle Roger 'll believe it, and they'll all believe it, and I can hold my face up again, and try to be good and happy. But you don't believe it, I see you don't. Nobody would. You think as they do—that I'm no good—no good."

She sobbed so loudly and cried so piteously, and shook so through all her poor maidenly frame, that he could not help but creep more closely to her. So near was he now, that he could have touched her with his outstretched hand. Still he forbore and did not do so.

"Will you swear it—swear that all this is true?" he asked, with intense earnestness of tone, as though his happiness, no less than hers, depended upon its being so, and his being able to believe that it was so. "Will you swear that——"

She broke in upon his question.

"I will swear that my last fault was to have met him in the wood that night, in order to bid him good-bye for ever. Were it otherwise, I never would have married you or anybody else. This I swear." She fell upon her knees. "As I believe there is a God in Heaven, I swear that all this is true!"

He touched her now, and drew her up from her knees.

"I believe you. You asked him not to marry you to anybody who was wicked or cruel. Cruel I fear I have been to you, but wicked, really wicked, I believe I have never been, and now I hope I never shall be. You are my wife, and I will try to make you happy. But I am not young, and I am beggared, and can do very little. Do you think you can ever get to love me?"

" Oh, yes, sir, because you are miserable. I think I can love anybody who is miserable. But—but—oh, sir, I love you now —now already!" she exclaimed, a rich, rising joy ringing through her voice— " because—because you have believed me!"

* * * * *

Half an hour later they were sitting together, husband and wife, side by side, he holding her hand in his.

" I was so frightened when you came in," she was saying, " and I rushed to that other door, thinking that somebody was forcing his way in from there. And I was all the more frightened because the night before last two men did come into that room, and I saw them, and screamed, and then they ran away."

" You saw them!" he exclaimed. " I heard yesterday that the house had been entered, and that the dining-room window had been opened, and that they had got in through there, but I did not know that they had come upstairs."

" Yes, but they did; and hearing a noise I got up and opened that door and saw them distinctly, and they saw me. And though they ran away, I was horribly frightened; for I could not help thinking that they had come to carry me away again, just as I was carried away in the wood."

" Poor child!" he said, tenderly, pressing her hand.

" Yes, and when you came in to-night, I thought it was the same men again as the night before last, and that they were coming for me, to carry me off—perhaps to murder me. Yes, to murder me. I thought that too. And they had masks on, which frightened me more; for the men who carried me off in the wood and rowed me in the boat that night, had masks also."

" Stay!" he said, starting forward, as

though something had suddenly struck him which it now seemed half strange to him he should not have thought of before. "Two men spoke to me in the park this morning, and accused me of carrying off a girl at Dipley——"

"Dipleydale," she said, correcting him.

"Dipleydale; of course it was Dipleydale. It's as clear as can be. They must be the men who did carry you off, and who came in here the night before last, and saw you and recognised you, and then concluded, because you were in my house, that they had been employed by me to do it."

"But they must have known that it was Lord Rendover."

"Not at all, Jessie," he said, smiling at her simplicity. "He would take care not to let them know who he was, any more than at first he let you know. They charged me to-day with employing them for the purpose, and threatened if, as they said, I would not come down handsome and buy them off, that they would see what the law would say to me."

He rose from his seat, leaving her awhile, and began pacing up and down the room in thought.

"Perfectly clear, perfectly clear," he said, going back to her again. "They are the very men whom he employed, the brutes who helped him. Now they want to find him out and use him in turn. And *I* can tell them, *I* can tell them!" he added, exultantly. "Jessie! Jessie! we both can be even with him yet!"

"But would it be well or wise?" she said, timidly. "I am your wife now, you know, and you would not like perhaps——"

"Right, right," he answered. "You are right, Jessie. I should not. Innocent as I know you to be, publicity would never do."

"I thought not," she said. "But how very strange! I know you believed me before; but is it not strange that you should so very soon have proof of part of what I told you being true?"

This too had not struck him as yet, till she thus pointed it out.

"Of course it is," he said, his eyes beaming with pleasure. "Of course it is a proof, and it is very, very strange. But I assure you, Jessie, I needed no proof. Indeed I believe you without."

"Yes, yes, I know you did," she said, hiding her face; "and that is why— why——"

"That is why you will try to love me?" he asked.

"Why I love you now, and shall always do so. I did not think that anybody would ever believe me." She clapped her hands just like a child. "Oh, to think that somebody believes me! And you will take me to Aunt Mary and Uncle Roger, and make them believe me, will you not; and everybody, everybody?"

"Yes, my dear, I will. But all in good time. Just let me think about that other point—about *him*, I mean. I must see young Carryngton about it. He's a sensible fellow, and an honourable man, and is the person most concerned in Rendover's reputation."

"What name did you say, please?" she asked.

"Carryngton. Percy Carryngton, Rendover's younger cousin."

"Do you know *him?*" she asked.

"Yes; do you?" he replied, quickly and almost a little angrily.

"I saw him once," she answered, timidly; "only once. He came down to the cottage one evening, and said he wanted to see his cousin, and he stayed two hours, and he was very kind, though I was afraid of him, and oh, I am so glad you know him!"

"Why are you so glad?"

Again she hid her face, but said quite as simply and honestly as she had said everything else,

"Because he will be able to tell you what I was like then. Oh, I was so frightened of him, and wanted him so much to go, though he was so kind and respectful. I am so, so glad you know him! Ask him about me. You will ask him about me, will you not?"

How thickly the proofs were coming of her goodness, her purity, her sufferings, her patience, her worth!

"Yes, if you like, Jessie. But I want to ask nobody. I believe you, because— because—who could disbelieve you? But we will both go and ask him. I must see him at once, if I can find him, and you shall come with me."

"Shall I? Oh, how delightful! Is he married, and shall I see his wife?"

The woman wanted to see a woman. Then alone could she feel that it was all right, and that she was thoroughly believed.

"No, he is not married. At least he was not when I saw him last. He is a bachelor. I hope he is in London, or in England, at any rate; for we must do nothing without consulting him. Probably he will want us to leave Rendover alone."

"And let us do so!" she said, imploringly. "I do not want to be revenged; do you?

Let us forgive him. Aunt Mary and Uncle Roger used to tell me we ought to forgive, and the Lord's Prayer says we ought, and I am sure we ought; ought we not?"

"Perhaps we ought, Jessie. But I must see Mr. Carryngton, and we must start for London to-morrow."

"And you will always believe me, and never doubt—never, never?"

"Always, Jessie. I would stake my life on your truth."

• Tears of joy rushed to her eyes, and she shed them on his breast. And then the silence of the night closed around them.

CHAPTER XI.

AN UNEXPECTED VISITOR.

How meanwhile had things been going on
with the newly married couple in Ranunculus Terrace, with the Percy Carryngton
whom Chichester Fleetwood imagined still
a bachelor, and his beautiful young wife?
Had all with them been unclouded sunshine,
and were they still as happy as when we
saw them, about two months ago?

Fortune rarely treats even her favourites
to unbroken calm and contentment; and if
we could suppose that she really has an
authoritative say in such matters, we should
hardly expect to find her doing so. Were
she indeed as intelligent as she is commonly
believed to be partial, should we not surely

anticipate her preparing for them somewhat chequered bliss, and infusing into
the sweets she gives that slight something
bitter which flavours life?

As the new year began to creep on,
Gertrude fancied that she traced in Percy's
manner an occasional irritation, or rather
perhaps a too evident attempt at suppressing
irritation, which she had never seen in it
before. He was just as loving as ever, just
as kind, just as dear. Nevertheless, if he
was not every now and then a trifle
petulant, it was more because he was
constantly striving to prevent himself from
being so than because he was free from any
inclination to be so. He was on the verge
of losing his temper over and over again, if
he never actually lost it.

In suppressing such inclinations considerable virtue is often required, and
Gertrude was not the woman to miss or to
undervalue so excellent and arduous an
exercise of the will. But she wholly failed
to conceive what reason there could be

either for the temptation or this resistance. She had never detected in him any trace of that terrible weakness, perilous in all circumstances, ruinous in domestic life, of being irritated periodically without any assignable motive. And when she came to rack her brains to discover a motive, sufficient or insufficient, she was more puzzled than ever.

At the same time she observed that, without growing less kind or less affectionate, he grew quieter and less cheerful. He would sit thinking, when they were together and in leisure moments, instead of telling her his thoughts and being anxious to arrive at hers. There was moreover, not unoften, what is called a cloud upon his brow. He looked bothered. Yet what could he be bothered about? Feeling satisfied that there was no real cause for it all, she feared as yet to allude to it, lest by so doing she should possibly make it worse.

Then she tried to persuade herself that it

was all her fancy. But this effort at self-
deception would not do. It was *not* her
fancy. The cloud was there and no mistake
about it.

Next she endeavoured to persuade herself that it was a peculiarity with men, and
common to them all. But she had seen too
many men, and had once known Percy himself to be too dissimilar from what he was
now, for this explanation to serve her any
better than the former one.

It began really to be a grief to her, for
the cloud upon his brow grew darker, and
became almost a settled one. Could it
possibly be that he found the new life
irksome and too full of restraints? Was he
unfitted for married life, or as yet not
broken into it? Was he pining for more
liberty? She could scarcely think this.
Darker and darker as might grow the
cloud, he loved her dearly; loved her, to
say the least of it, quite as much as ever.
Of this she felt certain. Moreover she knew
that she was not an exacting wife. He

might have gone into town, to his club or elsewhere, as much as ever he found necessary, and he would never have met from her anything but a smiling, happy face when he returned. Neither did he exercise this liberty half as much as he might have done. He left her but rarely. It was not that he was much away from her, but that he was not perfectly happy when he was with her, that caused her anxiety and sorrow.

Was he chafing under the simplicity of their way of living? Was that it? Was he regretting the old luxuries, the horses, the dinners, the social pleasures, which he had once had in such abundance? Did he find their living in lodgings difficult to endure, their two servants an annoyance, their five hundred a year a hindrance to his happiness?

No, no. This she would not believe. She would have been forced to despise him, if she had been forced to believe it. Nor were there any grounds for suspecting it.

He had never let fall a word which could justify such a supposition. He studied hard, and studied well, proving to her, whenever she shared in his studies, that she had not overrated his powers, but that he had an intellect considerably beyond hers; one which she could look up to and reverence. It was not when he was studying that the cloud was there. It was heaviest when he was unoccupied, especially when she caught him unawares and alone.

What could it be? She was already making up her mind to speak to him about it when an incident occurred which, without throwing any light upon his apparent depression of spirits, threatened to cast more than a temporary shadow over hers.

Percy had gone into town in the morning, a thing he very rarely did. He was to be home for luncheon, and Gertrude was to walk and meet him, so that he might have the last mile or so back home with her. It was a beautiful day, and she set out with a determination to ask him, as she hung upon his arm that morning, why he was so much altered, and if she was at all to blame for it.

When she was about a quarter of a mile from Ranunculus Terrace, on her way to meet him, a brougham, driven rapidly, suddenly pulled up at the kerb stone, close to her. She was already in rather a nervous mood, from her resolve to speak to Percy and the consciousness that the time for speaking to him was so near. She started. A lady was putting her head out of the window of the brougham, and addressing her. It was Mrs. Atwell Underhill.

Gertrude had not called upon that lady a second time. She felt the greatest aversion to doing so, and Percy had yielded to her feeling. They had been invited to dinner at Jessamine Lodge; but they had not gone, and it was by this time pretty well understood that visiting was at an end between the two houses. Atwell, of course, regarded Mrs. Percy Carryngton as only one woman more who was jealous of his wife's good looks, though Gertrude was herself infinitely lovelier. Between the two men the old friendship was still supposed to subsist, though as neither could enter the house of the other, their opportunities of seeing each other were not very frequent.

"How are you, Mrs. Carryngton?" said the liveliest of artificial voices. "What a time it is since we have seen each other! I am so glad to have met you! Wont you come and take a drive with me?"

"Thank you, very much," Gertrude replied, not yet quite recovered from the sudden start which she had had, "but I am on my way to meet Mr. Carryngton."

"Then let me take you. I will go in any direction you like."

"Thank you, but I really came out on purpose for a walk. I would much sooner walk. Besides, driving, I should go too far, and also run the chance of missing Mr. Carryngton."

"I think we should contrive to see him between us. But why do you never come near us? Do come! Mr. Carryngton looked in a few days ago, but we never see *you*."

This last announcement was so startling to. Gertrude that she felt the colour rise instantly to her face. She parried Godiva's other words as well and as briefly as she could, devoting herself chiefly to getting away from the brougham door as quickly as possible, and walking on. When, however, the carriage was out of sight, she turned round and walked rapidly home.

"Why did you not come to meet me, darling? I was so disappointed."

"I did start, to do so," she answered; "but when I had got a little way I did not feel well; indeed, I felt quite unequal to going any further, so I turned back."

After luncheon she was worse, and went upstairs and lay down on her bed. Percy sat by her side, tender and sympathizing. By-and-by, she seemed as though she had fallen asleep. Then he crept noiselessly out of the room, and left her.

But she was not asleep; and as soon as he quitted her side, she gave herself up entirely to the painful thoughts and feelings which had already worked her into a fever.

Could it really be true that Percy was going to Jessamine Lodge without her knowledge? Mrs. Atwell Underhill had said distinctly that he had been there only the other day, and it was quite certain that he had never mentioned it, and equally certain that it was an understood thing that they would go there no more, either of them. She believed Mrs. Underhill to be capable of any amount of falsehood; still the woman was not likely to tell a lie that could so easily be found out to be one. It seemed clear that Percy had been there, and had hidden his going from her, his wife.

Why had he gone? Surely Percy did not care for the woman? He had not gone in order to see *her*, and to see her without his wife's knowledge. It was too terrible

to think of; she would not believe it of
Percy; she would not believe it as happen-
ing to herself. It would make life utterly
valueless. It would in fact be an end of
life; after all the love she had given him,
after all the brave battle she had fought for
him, he could not—could not have acted
thus. She was too noble to recapitulate,
even to herself, all that she had done for
him, or to conjure up any picture of where
he now would have been but for her and
her magnanimity. But she could not altogether banish the consciousness that if now
he could permit any woman in the smallest
degree to come between him and her, he
was utterly undeserving of the belief and
love she had extended to him.

In about an hour and a half she heard
him creep into the room again. She closed
her eyes, for she had been crying, and she
did not want him to see that she had. He
fancied that she was still asleep, but he
came and took his old place at the bedside.

She had fully made up her mind what to

do. She was so firmly set in nobleness, that noble doing came to her as rapidly as though it came by instinct. She would tell him at once what she knew; she would not imitate his example of secrecy. Heaven knew that her whole heart was open to him. She would ask to be fully admitted into his.

" Percy!" she said, without opening her eyes.

" Yes, darling, I am here. Are you awake?"

" Yes." She stretched out her arm on the bed. " Give me your hand, Percy." She still spoke with her eyes shut. " You were at Mrs. Atwell Underhill's the other day, and you never told me."

He started.

"I was at Atwell Underhill's," he said, as though he wished to make a distinction. " Who told you that I was there?"

" She did. I met her this morning, and she told me then. It was that which made me feel poorly, and turn back home."

"I wonder how she knew. I did not think Atwell was so foolish as to tell her that I had been there."

"I think, Percy, he was quite right. I may be wrong; but I think husbands and wives should tell each other everything that happens to them after marriage. But was she not there?"

"There, when I called, Gertrude! Of course not. I should not have gone in at all, if she had been."

She opened her eyes now. Oh, how thankful she felt that she had rebutted, with all her faith and love, the suspicion which had tried so hard to get itself accepted by her, that he had been to Jessamine Lodge, chiefly out of a desire to see Mrs. Underhill.

But as she opened her eyes, she saw upon her husband's brow the cloud she had seen there so often of late, and she saw it lowering more darkly than she had ever seen it before. She jumped up from her reclining posture and looked earnestly at him. All

pain of her own, the pain arising from a
horrible doubt unsolved, such as she had
been suffering from for the last few hours,
was banished. There only remained the
pain of feeling that there was something he
had not thought fit to communicate to her,
but even this feeling entirely gave way
before the certainty that flashed upon her
that she was on the track of the cause—
whatever it might be—of all Percy's recent
want of spirits, fits of silence, and anxiety
of mien.

"Percy, there is something which worries
you, and has worried you for some time,
and it is connected with Atwell Underhill. I have noticed it for many weeks and
had fully made up my mind to mention it
to you to-day and ask you all about it,
and get you to tell me, when I met that
dreadful woman. Will you not trust your
wife?"

"Yes, darling, I will; and I only wish I
had told you before; but I could not bring
myself to do so. I thought perhaps the

bother would blow over, and that there would be no need to torment you with it. I owe all that I have to you, and I could not bear to tell you that I was in a money difficulty. That too was why I wanted to work and make something at once."

" But I thought you paid all your debts with the four hundred pounds? And what has Mr. Underhill got to do with it?"

" Everything. He is the principal person concerned."

He told her all that the reader knows, and just a little that the reader does not. This was to the effect that, neither Atwell nor he being able to pay the first instalment now overdue, they were trying to raise the money in some fresh way or other. They were both in the greatest perplexity, and it was necessary that they should see each other pretty often about it.

" I met him the other afternoon quite accidentally, and he begged me to go into his house, which we were close to, and look at some papers which he had to show me, connected with the subject. He said his wife was not there, and I am sure she was not."

"No doubt she was not. And she told me what she did—literally true though it was—to deceive me for a time and make mischief. But never mind that. Let us talk about the other matter."

They talked about it for a considerable time, and Percy had now to face the real facts of the case without flinching. Gertrude would hear of no schemes or expedients for staving off the evil day, or for gaining time. She would not listen to any possibility of Atwell's being made partner, or of something or other turning up. She saw but two things. One was that Mr. Underhill owed money, and Percy was security for its being paid. The other was that the former could not pay it, and that therefore the latter must.

"It's a great shame he cannot. What was she doing in a brougham to-day if he cannot? However, if he can't or wont, we must.   You say my money cannot be touched.   I am very sorry it cannot.   But there is your own hundred a year."

" But the stock is so low, that if I were to sell it, I should be literally throwing it away.   We get rather more than a hundred a year for it, and it would not sell for more than nine hundred pounds."

" Never mind.   You owe the money, and that is the only way of paying it, without involving yourself deeper.   You know I am right."

" Yes, you are, but I could not sell it without telling you."

" And you would not tell me?   Yes, I know; there lay the whole mischief.   But now it is easy.   Sell as much as ever you want for the present, and do it at once; to-morrow, if you can.   Tell him what you have done, and give him plainly to understand that you will do precisely the same next time, poor as you are, if he leaves you in the lurch at the end of the next six months."

As she advised, so it was done.   Indeed it was too clear to Percy that there was nothing else for him to do.   Poor Atwell, when he heard of it, was very much hurt, and swore that it should not happen again when the period for paying the next instalment came round, adding that of course he would pay Percy back as soon as ever he could.

" And I am sure he means what he says," said Percy, telling his wife what had passed between him and his friend.

" Perhaps he does, but the past does not encourage me to be sanguine.   That brougham was quite enough for me.   His wife will never let him be economical.   And, at any rate, being answerable for the money, we must be prepared to pay it, if he does not.   You know what I intend you to be some day, Percy ?   And when that day comes, I could not bear to think that anybody could say you ever had engaged to pay them money, and then failed to do so."

" But I am immensely sorry about it,

Gertrude. Even as it is, we are fifty pounds a year poorer than we were, and we were not very rich before."

"And perhaps in six months more we shall be fifty pounds a year poorer still. We must spend less; that is all. And if Mr. Underhill fails to do his duty, we must still do ours, be the result what it may. Should it become necessary, I will give in about your working a little, instead of devoting all your time to study. It will only make a difference of a few years," she added, with a proud confident smile. "You will begin to make your mark at forty-three instead of at forty."

How brave she was; how true, generous, inspiriting! As long as she could wear such a front as this, what troubles could daunt or even depress him? He had not felt so happy for weeks and weeks. The cloud had entirely disappeared from his brow. Their income was so much smaller, but his happiness was infinitely greater. He had no secret now, shut up from her scrutiny, and he never would withhold anything from her again.

"You will always tell me everything in future, will you not, Percy?"

"Yes, my own true wife! Always, always."

What a happy little dinner they had together! How he did enjoy his meerschaum after it! How he did enjoy her hand in his! How lovely she looked, how noble! And as she pushed his hair from off his brow with her delicate fingers, she vowed that he had never looked so handsome or so free from care before.

"Surely, that cab stopped at our house?"

"So I thought. Yes, listen; there's the front-door bell."

Who could it be? Presently in came Janet.

"Please, sir, there is a gentleman wishes to see you."

"Ask him his name, Janet."

Janet returned immediately.

"Please, sir, his name is Mr. Chichester Fleetwood."

CHAPTER XII.

ABOUT ten o'clock, two days after the event narrated at the end of the last chapter, a middle-aged man, tall and handsome, but rather greyer and more bent than he should have been for his years, came out of one of the houses in Ranunculus Terrace in the window of which was a card with the superscription, "Apartments to let, furnished." He was followed by a young girl, and together they walked to the very last house of all on the opposite side, the one already so well known to us. At the little gate a four-wheeled cab was already standing.

"Here they are!" exclaimed Gertrude, who had been impatiently waiting and watching for their arrival. "Are you ready, Percy?"

"I shall be in a moment. It is almost time we were starting."

If Chichester Fleetwood had been surprised, on arriving in London and making inquiries, to hear that Percy Carryngton was married and married to Gertrude Blessington, how much more surprised was Carryngton to hear that Chichester Fleetwood also had a wife and who the wife was!

"And she is with you?" Percy had said the evening Fleetwood had made his unexpected appearance. "Why did you not bring her in?"

"I did not like to do so without first seeing you."

"All right. Gertrude shall go and bring her in, and they can make each other's acquaintance whilst we talk matters over here."

They remained together in Percy's study, whilst Gertrude herself went out, dark night and cold as it was, and with her own hand led in the timid creature who was half hiding in the corner of the cab.

" Your husband and mine want to have a long talk together," she had said to her. "They are old friends, and we are to be new ones. But I am sure that in a very short time we shall know each other as well and be as fond of each other as they are."

And now Jessie knew that it was all right, and that she was believed; for it was a woman and a wife who was talking to her thus.

"And I hear you have got so much to tell me," Gertrude had continued, when she had placed Mrs. Fleetwood in a chair near the fire, and taken one close to her. "Do tell me; for I hear it is immensely interesting. You must not think it is the first time I have heard of you. Percy and I have often talked of you, and we once made a journey on purpose to see you. But I will tell you all about that after. You must tell me first all you have got to say; for Percy says it is so exciting."

When, nearly an hour later, the two men had joined them, they found them already apparently on the very best of terms. Gertrude had put her visitor quite at ease, and had heard from her all or, at any rate, nearly all that the reader knows. It was quite evident that both women had been crying, but not tears of sorrow.

Mr. and Mrs. Carryngton had no spare room to offer to their visitors; but it was arranged that Janet should run out and take a couple of rooms for them over the way, and they were to come and dine and make themselves at home generally during their stay, with Percy and Gertrude.

"It is out of the way and quiet, and you will see nobody, which I dare say is what you want just at present," said Percy.

"And you will be near to us," added Gertrude; "which is still better. And you will ask me for everything you want, Mrs. Fleetwood, will you not?"

"I am so glad," said Percy to his wife that same night, when they were again alone, " that Fleetwood came straight to me. It really was very sensible and considerate of him to do so, considering the provocation they both were under to be even with Rendover at once."

" But how could they do anything, my dear," asked Gertrude, " now that Jessie is his wife? It would never have done to make a scandal."

" Of course not, and he sees that clearly enough. Still it was very good of him to come and consult me, little knowing that I have just about as much reason to love Rendover as he has, but supposing all the time that I had every interest in getting my cousin out of a scrape."

" And you have come to the conclusion that it is much better to do nothing at all in the matter?"

" Just so. And he seems so well satisfied with the state of affairs, and is so much attached to Jessie, that he has no desire to do anything."

" And I am sure she quite forgives Rendover. Oh, how nice and good she is, and how good, how good she must have been all along! Poor dear! I do love her so; I love her already. And she has such nice quiet manners, and speaks very prettily too, and is so modest and humble."

"Isn't she? She only wants a little female society."

"I am sure she may have as much of mine as ever she likes, if that will be any good to her."

"It will be all the good in the world," answered Percy, "and I am so delighted to hear you say so; and Fleetwood will be so grateful. He tells me that the principal thing she wants to do, is to go down with him to Dipleydale and see her aunt and uncle, and prove to them that she is married and respectable, and good. She wants to go at once."

"And she is quite right, and I honour her all the more for it. Why should they not go at once? And why?—but I forgot."

"You meant—why should we not go

with him? Only you think we cannot afford it," said Percy, divining both her thoughts.

" I did. What do you think? Can we? They would both like it so much; and I am sure it would be an immense comfort and encouragement to her."

It was at last settled between them that they must contrive to afford it, and that they would go. That was the meaning of the cab standing this morning at their door, of Mr. and Mrs. Fleetwood hurrying across, and of Gertrude and Percy being ready to accompany them.

The journey to Dipleydale was a long and rather a wet one; but by the time they got there, the weather had taken up, and it was a bright March day, with a dash of coming April in it. Poor Jessie was in a fever of conflicting emotions. Her love for her husband, her worship for Gertrude, her reverence for Mr. Carryngton, had now to be swollen by other and still more exciting sensations. She wondered if people would recognise her. She hoped they would. Then she hoped they would not. She wanted to be seen; but when there came the chance of being seen she shrank from it. Her real innermost desire was for the Dipleydale people to behold her on her husband's arm. Yet, when anybody approached whom she recognised, and who she imagined would recognise her, she went and walked by Gertrude, and almost hid herself behind Gertrude's skirts. '

If she could only have mustered up courage to go into Britton's lending library, where she used to get all those novels, and to ask them all three to go in with her! The day after to-morrow would be Sunday. She wondered if they might all stay and go to Uskmoor church to service. Oh, how often, during the last sixteen months, she had wished herself there—back, even there! But all was well now. That terrible time was past for ever.

They were to go up to Netwold Farm that very afternoon, starting not from

Dipleydale, but from Diplcymouth, whither their conveyance had first brought them, and where they had put up at an unpretending but comfortable English country inn. They started about half-past three, and were to ascend the right bank of the stream through the woods. Percy had gone back to the inn to borrow a stouter stick, and now came running after them.

"Do you know whom I just caught sight of?" he said, when he overtook them. "At least I feel pretty sure it was he."

"Who, Percy?" asked his wife.

"I don't suppose you ever saw him, my dear; but Mr. Fleetwood probably has seen him often. Do you remember Thornton, Fleetwood? Rendover's servant, I mean?"

"Fellow with red hair; looked like a wig. Of course, I remember him."

"And so do I," said Jessie, clinging to her husband's arm and speaking in a lower tone. "I hope *he* is not here."

"Thornton? Why not, my child?" he asked.

"No; Lord Rendover himself, I mean. And yet—yet I *should* like him to see me with you."

"If he is here, he *shall* see you with me. But that is very improbable. Are you sure it was he, Carryngton?"

"Not sure; but it was uncommonly like him. I caught such a hasty glimpse of him that I may be quite mistaken."

"Probably you are. What could he be doing here?"

"They must have carried me all down here," whispered Jessie to Gertrude. "I did not see anything; but they must have kept along this path, because there is no other. But how or where they got me into the boat, I don't know."

"How awful it must have been! I wonder you were not driven mad."

"Or that I did not die of fright. But I was unconscious most of the time. All that I knew was that I was helpless, and that it was quite dark, and there was a great noise of the stream, and then a greater

noise of the sea, for there had been a tre-
mendous storm. And then when I got
more conscious and tried to scream, they
prevented me in some way or other, and
then I heard nothing, but only felt
motion."

" How swollen the stream seems to-day,
after all the rain. Was it more so then?"
asked Gertrude.

" Perhaps not more, but as much, I
think. Indeed I never saw it fuller than it
is this afternoon. But it is always fullest
in spring."

"And how slippery it is! I think I
must have Percy's arm. They are always
dropping behind and talking together, those
husbands of ours. But then they know we
like to be together."

" And do you—can you—really love me,
Mrs. Carryngton?"

" You know I do, and dearly. But I
will not, if you call me Mrs. Carryngton."

" I shall get accustomed to call you
Gertrude by-and-bye; but I am afraid and

ashamed a little, you know. But how can you love me? I am so foolish, and stupid, and ignorant, and so different from you. I know nothing, and you know everything. Do you think you will ever be able to make me at all like you, so that Mr. Fleetwood shall think so and need not be ashamed of me?"

"He cannot be that now. Indeed, he is proud of you, and I know it; and so he ought to be. There! I was nearly down."

"It was just like this that night. I nearly slipped over two or three times on my way from the farm to meet him, when I meant to say good-bye to him for ever. But that was on the other side of the stream altogether, and much higher up. I will show it you when we get there."

"Then was it on the other side of the stream that they seized hold of you?"

"No, on this. I had agreed to meet him on the other side, just by a litle narrow stone bridge, which we shall come to by-and-by, and shall have to cross; for there the path up the stream is only on the other side, just as below the bridge it is only on this side."

" Then you had crossed the bridge and had come to this side ?"

" Yes; because immediately below the bridge the stream gets narrower and swifter, and falls over a ledge of rock into a sort of basin, that it makes for itself by falling, you understand. Such a lot of water as there is! and such a rush! It looks as if it were all boiling and hissing. It will be splendid to-day, from there being so much water; and you will see it."

" And what a noise it must make."

" That was just the reason why we crossed the bridge. I was going to tell you. We crossed it and came to this side, and went lower down in order to get away from the noise of the water, for we could not hear each other speak on account of it. I will show you the exact spot when we get there. But you will hear something of the roar long before we reach it."

"And you never suspected for a moment what was coming?"

"I had not an atom of fear. I was only thinking how I could best give him back the things, and say good-bye, and make him understand perfectly that I would never see him again. I was full of all that. I never dreamed of violence. And it was all done in a second. He turned away from me towards the bridge and whistled; and then I was alarmed, and suspected something; but not before. But the instant I turned to run in the opposite direction—down the road, towards here, you understand—I was stopped. I had rushed straight into the men's arms."

"How treacherous! Of course he had done it all on purpose—the turning, and the whistling across the bridge in order to deceive you."

"Of course he had. Oh! it was horrible. It makes me tremble all over, even now, when I think of it. How can men be so cruel?"

Gertrude took her hand, and they walked on a little in silence. The trees were still bare of buds, but the underwood was beginning to throw out tentative shoots and climbers, and the moss around the old roots and knotted trunks looked fresh and moist and green, and the primrose leaves had made themselves very visible again, and would soon let out from prison life their sweet pale golden flowers.

" Is not this glorious?" called out Percy from behind them. "And are we not more than repaid for coming by this one walk alone?"

The two ladies halted, and then all the four travellers were together.

" And look at the sea, through there!" said Jessie. " We begin to have a view of it, even now. But it grows much finer as you get higher up. I must show you the view I used to have from my little bedroom window at home."

Thank Heaven! she could talk of home once more without either a blush or a tear!

" I should like to see it so much," said

her husband. "Will you show it to me, Jessie, as well?"

"Of course I will; but I want Mrs. Carryngton to see it particularly."

"And I will. Oh! how lovely all this is!"

"But you should see it in summer, when all the leaves are on the trees. You cannot tell how beautiful it is."

Again they were walking two-and-two; husband and wife, husband and wife; for the path grew steeper and more slippery. Percy and Gertrude walked on in front, Fleetwood and Jessie following at a very short distance. She was telling him anew what she had told him before, and what she had just been trying to describe to Mrs. Carryngton.

"I think I hear the roar of the fall now," said the latter, turning her head round; "do I not?"

Jessie stood a moment and listened attentively.

"Yes, that must be it. We shall be close to it before long."

They walked on again, the noise growing more distinct as they did so.

"We shall shortly be on the very spot where I was carried off," whispered Jessie. "Shall I point it out to them?"

"What a deafening noise! How swollen the stream is!"

"And see, there is the little bridge!"

"It was just here that they did it. Yes, that is the bridge. Oh, how I remember it all!"

"Look! there are some people the other side of it. And see, see!"

It was Percy who had spoken. They all looked in the direction in which he pointed. There were three men the other side of the little stone bridge; two of them roughly dressed, like common working men, the third dressed like a gentleman. The former were evidently not only attempting to bar his passage across it, but seemed to be trying to seize him.

"By Jove! he's going to try to leap the stream. Hi! Stop! stop!"

But as he spoke, the man took his spring. It was a fine, difficult jump, but for an active person, not an impossible one. One of the two men slightly balked him in it, and consequently he threw too much of his spring into height and too little into breadth. At the same time too, he swerved slightly from the direction he had meant to take.

" He'll do it."

" He's short; he'll fall in the water."

He did neither. The balk and the consequent swerve had told. The lappets of his coat too had been flung out by his spring and by the air combined, and caught in the extreme point of a thick but dead and already splintered branch that stretched right over the stream. The bough cracked audibly, even amid the din of the torrent. It did not break, however, but held him out at arm's length in mid air, and straight above the deep basin of seething waters.

" It's he!—it's he!" shrieked Jessie.

19—2

"As I live it's Rendover!" exclaimed Percy.

"Save him! Save him! One of you— oh, save him!"

"We couldn't, an' we would," shouted back one of the men from the other side of the bridge. "He's done for hisself now."

They all looked at him, and he at them. He recognised them all—those whom he had plotted and toiled to injure—those who, for all that, would have saved him now— and they could not!

Then came a fresh crackling sound— a splintering—a snapping—the shrieks of the women—and the rotten branch dropped with its burden into the abyss of plunging foam. A dull, heavy splash, and then again only the roar of the tumbling torrent.

Their cheeks were pale and their lips were glued with horror. But they thought of the dread words which will keep their sway over men's hearts till wrong shall cease to be done on earth by the strong and the cruel:—

" Vengeance is Mine! saith the Lord. I will repay."

* * * * *

The reader who has followed the story carefully throughout will easily understand, if indeed he have not already guessed, how Lord Rendover came to be in the Dipley-dale woods when Percy and Gertrude, Fleetwood and Jessie, were making their way up the stream to Netwold Farm.

When Abraham Coggett found himself once more in the hands of the men against whom he had turned informer and given damning evidence, he threw himself entirely on their mercy, and became just as much their instrument as, since the night of the first burglary at Fleetwood Manse, he had been Lord Rendover's. He made a clear breast of it, and told them everything; and was just as ready to betray Rendover into their clutches as he had betrayed them into his.

Accordingly, in obedience to their designs, he wrote three or four successive letters to his master, the tenor of which was that he was at last on the track of the escaped felons. He had to be very cautious, he wrote, but he would take care that they should not escape. Then came a letter to Lord Rendover, informing him that they were in communication with Chichester Fleetwood and Jessie, whom by some means or other, unknown to the writer, they had contrived to get at.

The next communication of the supposed spy was that he had overheard a conversation between them and Fleetwood in the park, in which it had been arranged that the two men should go down to Dipleydale, see Roger Barfoot and his wife, and complete the evidence against their common enemy.

"They will be there on Friday or Saturday," he wrote. "I too will go down there, and will set the police after them. If your lordship also would go down, I think it would be better, as I am afraid of its failing without your lordship's help."

Rendover needed no inciting. The news that the men whom he had employed in the abduction were in communication with Jessie, who could tell them everything, and with Fleetwood who would of course strain every nerve to have his revenge, filled him with alarm. He started at once for Dipley-dale. On arriving there he did not descend to Dipleymouth at once, but went straight up to Netwold Farm to look about him and see if there were any signs of the old people being already in communication with Speke and Stebbins. He was coming back again from the inspection, by the very road which Jessie had taken on the fatal night, and with the intention of now going to Dipleymouth, where he hoped to find his servant Thornton and the police.

Arrived at the bridge, the men who had been lying in wait for him the whole day, and who were quite prepared to lie in wait for him the whole of the next, sprang out upon him. Their object was to seize him and not to let him go till he had bought off

their silence with a sufficient sum, or till
they had handed him over to justice, even if
by so doing they would have to share his fate.

Seeing them spring out upon him, and
at once attempt to seize him, he conjectured
that their object was violence, and violence
only—the physical revenge which comes
swiftest and easiest to uncultivated natures.
How he strove to escape it and so preserve
his freedom for future use against them we
have seen.

His body of course was found, but with
the life battered out of it by the tumbling
torrent and the resisting rocks.

Four months had passed away, and it
was the very height and flush of summer
through the length and breadth of beautiful
England.   Never had the country looked
richer or lovelier, and Carryngton Manor
might have challenged any other domain in
the land to a show of beauty and fertility.
It was not full of guests, but there was a
fair number, among whom may be named
Mr. and Mrs. Chichester Fleetwood, Squire

Blessington and his wife, and Mrs. Grantley Morris. The host and hostess were Percy and Gertrude Carryngton. No will of the deceased nobleman could be found, and Percy was his heir-at-law.

Roger Barfoot and Aunt Mary are still at Netwold Farm, and still go to Uskmoor church every Sunday. But their farm is their own, and they are surrounded with every comfort that can crown a life of honourable but simple rural labour. They talk of Jessie every night of their lives, and remember her every night, and now with pride and comfort, in their prayers. They only know that she is honestly married, and this their limited knowledge is as much as is known by either Dipleymouth or Dipley-dale. These worthy twin little villages have also quite recanted their hasty opinion, and are declaring that Jessie has promised to come down in the autumn with her grand husband, and see the old people at Netwold. And there never was such another pretty, lucky lass in this world.

They are almost right. Mrs. Fleetwood
is thoroughly happy, and so is her husband.
She has been constantly with Mrs. Carryngton and Mrs. Morris, who have taken
infinite pains with her, and are succeeding
admirably in putting her at ease among,
and so fitting her for, that society which she
will end by adorning with her grace as she
now improves it by her virtue.   Both ladies
love her as a sister.   Carryngton insists on
repaying Fleetwood the money which Rendover forced him to spend at Leverstoke
and over the petition.   He swears it is a
debt of honour on the Carryngton estate;
and its repayment will give the disappointed
candidate a handsome income for life.

Percy has also paid the whole of Atwell
Underhill's debt to the insurance company.
It was Gertrude's own suggestion. Rigidly
just and prudent as she was in the days of
Ranunculus Terrace and limited means, she
shows herself in this her hour of altered
fortune, still just but overflowingly generous.   Poor Atwell is not yet made a

partner, and I begin to fear he never will
be. He is looking older and depressed.
Godiva, too, has turned the corner, and is,
I hear, taking to powder, unguents, and
their kindred artifices for preserving the
beauty that is doomed. He, however, does
not see the change, but still firmly believes
that each fresh woman who makes his wife's
acquaintance and then refuses to continue
it, is jealous of her good looks. If he
thought otherwise, what a miserable fellow
he would be!

"I have just received this letter from
America," says Percy, coming out of his
library—very different from the little room
in their lodgings—and going up to Gertrude,
who was leaning over the balustrades of
the principal terrace, watching the sun set
over the splendid expanse of English wood-
land. "Those two fellows have arrived
safely, and promise to become honest citizens
and earn their bread like honest men. But
the other scamp—Rendover's servant that
was—died on the passage."

At this moment up came Squire Blessington, who is now quite reconciled to his
daughter and his son-in-law; the world, in
this respect, having followed his example;
but Mrs. Grantley Morris, with her usual
instinct, felt sure that Percy was saying
something of a private nature to his wife,
and did not want to be disturbed. So she
too approached and tried to lead the squire
away.

" I want to join Mr. and Mrs. Fleetwood,
will you take me, Mr. Blessington? See!
they are by the water side."

" By all means, Mrs. Morris. Let us go."

" How happy they all seem," said Percy.

" Yes, I think they do, and we must try
always to make them so."

" And do you know, Gertrude, that
people are saying it is a pity the title
should die out, and I have received an intimation that it will be renewed in my
favour, if I care for it."

" But you do not, I am sure. So far, it
has been dishonoured, however few people

know it.   As for you—or may I say
us?"

"Yes, my darling! for I am nothing
without you!"

"As for us—we have done nothing to
deserve it, as yet. If some day or other,
the voice of our countrymen shall declare
that we merit some token of their approbation, not for carpet manufacturing, nor
for buying boroughs or even counties, but
for some benefit wrought for them and for
mankind, it will then be time enough to
consider the offer."

"And are we to do some such thing for
mankind?" he asked, smiling.

"At any rate," she answered, "we are to
try."

Let us leave them then to their efforts.
Content shall I be if I have so far succeeded
in mine, that the good wishes of my readers
accompany them. The aim of every
sincere writer must be either to inculcate
truth or to incite to virtue. The former
scarcely comes within the province of the

novelist. All the more earnestly, therefore, should he devote himself to the latter.
Amusement is his vehicle, and I have
availed myself of it to the best of my
ability. But I trust that if any have been
entertained, they have also been warmed
to a closer love for good, and a still firmer
faith in its efficacy, by the perusal of
" Jessie's Expiation."

END OF VOL. III.

www.ingramcontent.com/pod-product-compliance
Lightning Source LLC
Chambersburg PA
CBHW060555030726
47498CB00005B/1400